BLADE

OF

FIRE

L.M. PRESTON

Editor: Cindy Davis

Proof Reader: Dawn Yacovetta

Cover Design by We've Got You Covered. All Rights Reserved.

All Rights Reserved.

ISBN: Paperback: 978-1-7379476-6-0
ISBN: Ebook: 978-1-7379476-5-3

Published by Phenomenal One Press

A Phenomenal One Press publication, December 20th, 2022

www.phenomenalonepress.com

This series is dedicated to my four kids.

You each have your own superpowers within you. We are all survivors and have been through some awesome adventures together. You fuel my characters and give me endless material. You are a major encouragement to keep writing, and I couldn't ask for a better support team for allowing me to read my stories to you, asking you for names of my characters, or to show me martial arts moves while staging live-action sparring exercises.

To my husband who keeps pushing me to be more creative and makes sure I don't give up.

Thanks to God for giving me this anxious energy to create and tenacious spirit of positivity with an active imagination.

To my devoted Beta Reader, my daughter, and Proofreader, Dawn.

To my editor, Cindy Davis, who's been my best support in my art.

Chapter 1

The waters were freezing. Mermaids with spears swarmed around him. Reece swam toward them to block them from attacking the van he'd broken out of after freeing his family from its confines. The other mermaid who had attacked – he'd killed her then watched her body sink as the others approached. One grabbed him from behind and then covered his head to disorient him so they could chain his arms. Killing the mermaid general was a diversion to draw them away from his family in hopes of their rescue, as Megan promised.

Reece couldn't hold his breath much longer. He was being pulled deeper into the sea by chains that spread his arms so wide he thought they may get torn off. The pain was excruciating but did nothing to distract him from the anger that boiled deep inside. The mermen were furious at him, but not enough to kill him as he'd hoped. The sack they'd placed over his head loosened then floated off.

He twisted from right to left to count how many surrounded him. They didn't resemble the Merpeople he remembered from the animated movies he and his twin watched in childhood. These had thick green-scaled legs with finned feet. Their faces appeared human but were artfully adorned with unique, colorful scales. Those multi-colored scales fanned from their lips to the temples. Reece felt dizzy from staring at their hair. It swayed with the sea's current and was intertwined with strings of multi-colored seaweed. Their eyes were strange as they weren't a single hue but changed with the various colors reflecting the wave movements, constantly fluctuating with the hypnotic flow of the sea's undercurrent.

He suspected they no longer trusted him around their women. One of the mermen held up his arm, keeping the mermaids with their pitched-forked weapons at bay. He'd seen them use hand gestures and sharp words to retreat to communicate when he attacked the warrior mermaid who tried to restrain him. Their language was melodic and sounded like music within the caress of the waves. The mermaids were different from the men. They had full hips and tail fins of beautifully unique colors that complemented the various tones of their bare humanlike green skin. Those fins also held sharp shell-like claws that whipped to tear at his skin when they felt threatened.

His twin sister Rei had been fascinated with anything unworldly based on fairy tales, but Reece found it boring. Now he wished he'd paid more attention to her stories. These creatures would drown him in the clear waters of the sea. Reece shook his head to erase the accident that crashed his family's van into the cold waters. He hoped his attempt at trying to save his family had worked. He didn't know if he'd succeeded. All he knew was that the Merpeople didn't throw more spears into the van once they had him. Reece thought that would pay his debt to the evilest creature he could ever conceive – Megan.

Maybe he should open his mouth and let the water rush in, ending it all and freeing him from the devil's bargain he'd made with the two-faced girl. Megan had seemed innocent. As a Rumpelstiltskin, there was no benevolent bone within her manipulative magic body. He should have killed her when he had the chance. Reece couldn't reverse Megan's threats if she were dead. The vixen had an army of people who owed her favors, were magically bound to her, and supported her cause. Reece wanted nothing to do with it.

A mermaid's sharp spear pierced his shoulder. Another warrior merman snatched it out. Reece almost opened his mouth to growl in his pain.

The merman on his left yanked the thick chain harder; its bluish-green glow hinted at the magic within the restraint that contained Reece's strength. Reece knew they were ticked off because he'd stabbed their mermaid general. He smiled at one of the mermen and licked his lips to taunt him as he remembered biting the mermaid and sucking at the ancient blood that was left. Maybe consuming her blood helped him to sustain the depths of the sea.

Reece tugged at the chains to try their strength. He was glad the enchanted bind worked on him. Many times, Reece had attempted to harm himself. He'd been infected, changed, and cursed by someone he loved. Now he wondered if it was love or the engineered vamp's way of playing with her food. Every time he thought about her, his heart clenched before trembling with a sharp stab of betrayal. He was supposed to be enjoying his summer in his second year of high school. Instead, his head sagged to the side at the punch of a merman. Nothing had been the same since they'd moved to this mockery of Newport, which had been a nightmare.

He tried to calm his pain and anger by watching the radiant fish in the depths of blue. They were beautiful colors of blue, green, and yellow. The formation in which they swam made Reece narrow his gaze. They seemed in perfect sync with the mermen, as though the mermen directed them in formation to add another layer of security to keep him contained. The fish darted in and out, stopping briefly to swivel and gaze at Reece. A larger fish of blue opened its mouth, and Reece pulled back from its bared teeth. It snapped at his skin, pinching him. The fish's eyes grew wide, then filled with a black substance. Its body stiffened, and it wavered, then rolled over as it died. One of the mermen had been watching. Reece smirked at its stricken expression – fear was usually never well hidden. As they drew closer, the cluster of them scurried in a burst of activity before disappearing.

Reece couldn't hold his breath any longer. He'd been a good swimmer and could even hold his breath for more extended periods, but even he knew his new body was different now. He relaxed his mouth, and the saltiness of seawater flooded it, forcing it open. The suffocating sensation of drowning was miserable. It was a violation of your body, from the mouth, which would sustain you or allow you to voice your objection. The painful sharp gushing of water invaded his esophagus. The salt felt like shards of glass going down his throat. Still, Reece refused to close his eyes. His body rejected the water when he tried to inhale it and fought to purge it from his lungs.

They were taking him to a bubble, a dome of air that pushed back the raging waters of the sea. Part of him didn't want to go there – he didn't want to survive this. His belly was stuffed full of water. He'd felt the cramps of it creating small tears in the walls of his stomach. Would it happen? Would he be able to die?

The mermen swam faster, and Reece's eyes started to close. Waves smacked against his bare chest, and the consuming water drummed at his ears. The domed air pocket had sand the color of a dark navy blue sprinkled with gold. The chains released him. A cold pressure on his back from some weapon threw his body forward. He landed facedown inside the air-filled dome's soft navy gold-flecked sand. A gasp escaped from his mouth. The chain given to him to keep his thirst for magical blood under control had seeped into his skin, protecting itself and him from the effects of its release. Unfortunately, the bracelet Megan gave him to track his movements was still visible. She told him it would stay with him until he gained entrance to the fortress of their Overlord. Reece wanted it off.

His body betrayed him again. The only way he could rid himself of it was to die, which wasn't happening today. Sharp cramps forced him to bend over. Reece coughed and then heaved out the water. The vomiting continued with his stomach rumbling at the beginning of a new heave. He guessed the infection wouldn't let him drown even if he tried.

Reece braced his hands on his knees and vomited over and over again.

"You're alive?"

His body was recovering but still weak. Reece raised a trembling hand to his mouth and wiped away the remnants of water. His dark hair covered his face, and he wondered if lifting its heaviness from the pain throbbing at his temples was worth it. He wiped his forehead and grasped his straight black hair, pulling it away from his face. Lifting his chin, he clashed eyes with a tall, dark-skinned kid he remembered from his high school football team.

"I'm Trey. Jeb sent me to get you."

Chapter 2

Reece looked up at the bubble above, a barrier that separated the heaviness of the sea from the bottom of a mountain from black lava rock that had formed a cave with giant carved statues of mermaids with sharp teeth and finned ears on either side of the cave's entrance.

Reece stood his full six foot four inches to look down at Trey. He fisted his hands at his sides and exhaled to calm his anger at not being spared the freedom of death. "How do you know Jeb?" Reece frowned, studying the movement of the Soul Thief in front of him.

Jeb had saved him from himself, and Reece was forever indebted to him, to the Vigilant. But the Soul Warriors were pawns to the master of this place – The Void – a universe for magical beings created by the Fallen Angels who fathered and sparked the magic that made this world. They were humans who sold their souls to the Overlord, becoming the hidden police force for magical creatures. It was an unseen world that Reece hadn't known about until he'd fallen in love with one of them. That meant Trey could be an enemy.

"I am a Vigilant Ally." Trey crossed his arms. "I had to kill many of the other Soul Warriors to get here to you, and find a place for you to recover before I leave."

"If you are already at the Overlord's domain, why did he need me to follow through with Megan's threat? I was captured at the risk of the lives of my family. My parents and siblings may die because I'm here."

"Because there are more ways into his domain than this one. I can't get into his castle since I don't have the clearance. I killed many to get here to meet you." Trey pointed at Reece. "The mermen who bought you here fiercely protect this entrance from both magicals and the Overlord. Jeb's negotiation with those who are human sympathizers is the only reason the small group of rebels was able to bring you here before they were killed or captured by their kind. Fish people are a special kind of evil when torturing traitors and defending what they think is theirs." Trey lifted an eyebrow. "I heard you killed one of their generals."

Reece sighed. "I thought they were working for Megan."

"It's complicated, but they answer to no one."

His chest was naked, and his jeans were torn, exposing his lower legs, but the necklace that contained his unpredictable powers, remained hidden under his skin.

Finally, he felt the itch of it as it shifted. The necklace rose from his bronze skin. The chain of silver, the ruby crystal, long and sleek, came to a point.

"Are you strong enough to remove it? I cannot."

Trey narrowed his eyes. "What will happen?"

"I will change, and if you are strong enough to defend yourself against my hunger, then put it back on me."

"But you are strong without it? You had eight mermen

escorting you and holding you with their Chains of the Sea Dragon Teeth. That is powerful magic, and it barely contained you. Not only that – it couldn't be detected. You are the ultimate weapon for the Vigilant – and for Megan."

"Are you scared?" Reece smirked. The dark side of him killed without thought or hesitation. In those moments, Reece had no control. Some part of him wanted to survive and felt threatened.

"No, but I'm not stupid. If we go further, you will have to act human and never reveal your strength until you get close to Cyrillus. The Vigilant and I need you to find a better entrance for the Vigilant."

"Well, one is the sea – how did you get to the Overlord's domain?"

"The Kelpies."

"So, the only other way is through the sea, fighting the Merpeople and a mist horse demon who likes to be a woman?"

"Unless you know another way." Trey stepped closer and put his hand on his waist to remove the handcuffs that dangled from them.

"Wait, you are binding my hands?" Reece stepped back. He knew another way in but had to find it. He had no way of doing that if he was imprisoned.

"Of course I am. You think it wouldn't be suspicious if you weren't?" Trey smirked. "What's with the bracelet?"

"Megan put it on me."

Trey frowned. "I can get it off."

"She said it won't come off until I am here – or dead."

Trey's goldish bronze ring held a blue stone like the one Reece had touched once while trying to remove it from his brother.

Reece stumbled back, remembering the hellish visions that came from the ring. "What's in the ring? Don't touch me with that."

"The ring is attached to me – my curse. It gives me dark magic infusions and allows me to overpower magical beings and some magic talismans. It's bound to the devil as you know it. My blood is tied to the damned, and their magic travels through other Soul Warriors and me for the Overlord to siphon without the curse that comes with it. We are the ones that will be doomed into the lake of fire. The Overlord benefits from us being the middlemen."

Trey's hand was encased in the bluish glow of the ring. "I won't hurt you, but the removal of this bracelet might sting. It's a Vedisti-bead-gold from a stone dragon. I've removed objects made of it before."

Reluctantly, Reece extended his arm. Trey's hand covered the bracelet and flinched. Reece jumped at the shock of energy, followed by a burn that turned his veins dark.

"Ahh!" He was poisoned and weak as his magic within seemed to turn dark, dry, and brittle. He fell to his knees, but Trey didn't release him.

"Stop moving," Trey ground out, "I am taking the darkness from you. If you struggle, the transfer won't complete."

Reece relaxed, concentrating on his breathing and trying to block out the shocks of needles that burned in his blood.

"There. It's gone."

Reece opened his eyes to Trey's pensive gaze.

"You are different. I hope it's good."

"Well, I don't know yet." Reece jerked his hand from Trey's and stood.

"Time for the biggest act of your life. Don't blow it — your family's lives depend on it."

What life? Reece hadn't felt alive in a while. He wasn't alive; he existed for his mistakes, betrayals, and revenge. He was a monster who constantly warred with itself. His vampire and angelic halves were fighting for control, leaving the sliver of humanity Reece had gone, becoming a fickle balance.

Reece eyed the cave behind Trey. The small sandy opening in the bubble was the only passage to the dark gateway that was the arched entrance of the cave. It was large enough for something giant to fit through, but the darkness hung on its opening, not giving way to any hint of what was within. Trey led, and Reece followed like the fool he was.

Chapter 3

Once they entered the massive cave, a chill surrounded Reece's body as though the dark opening was more than a passage, but a transference to another place. His body felt intact when stepping through the archway of the cave, he had to push against the darkness as though it was a thick gel substance. It was unsettling, and Reece shook it off once his foot touched the firm rock surface inside. He swallowed and squinted at the scattering of lights within the cave to process what he was seeing. The blinking lights within it were eyes. "It's looking at us?"

Reece walked on the sand that gathered on the rock floor of the cave. It was dark, dry, and showed no signs of being a barrier to the bottom of the sea. The sand barely protected his bare feet from the sharply pointed pieces of rock that protruded in various places within the sand-swept space.

Trey chuckled. "They are like fireflies; only, the dark center is a stinger."

"What happens if they sting someone?"

"You swell up and turn green; but mostly, they're harmless."

"Why aren't they attacking?"

"They don't like my blood. If a Soul Thief or Trainer gets

stung or bit by a Vampire or a magical, our blood has certain effects. It kills them by poison or causes them to become addicted to us until they over-consume and overdose."

"But they aren't attacking me." Reece frowned at one, noting how it shivered and its small spine bowed as if it feared them.

"Maybe they sense your blood is also tainted. Some creatures know when they are around a predator – a poison."

Reece shut his mouth. There was much about his new body he didn't know. He was poison, the well-hidden kind. The hunger within him teased beneath his surface. Blood, magic, power it sought to consume.

Jeb had tried to study him like some untamed specimen he was afraid to let loose on the world. Until he realized he could use Reece's curse to save the magicals, the humans on the Earth Realm that had no idea they were in danger. Then Reece could destroy the devices of the two most potent magicals in The Void. Reece didn't think he was up for it anymore. He'd become afraid of himself and what he could do to someone as he discovered what new abilities had developed with his transformation into the creature he'd become. Reece didn't know if he was magical or not – he knew he was an abomination to them and humankind.

They passed through the cave to a circular door with a long handle. Trey moved it counterclockwise and then pushed it in to move it in the opposite direction. The door opened, and they entered a dark hallway encased in a metal woven with multi-colored threads of gold, silver, and green that cast a warm glow on the passage.

"What kind of metal is this?"

"A metal the forefathers of this place came here to mine. It can dim the magic energy of any being, and the longer someone's within its vicinity, the weaker they become. It's a security measure."

"How did you make it here?"

Trey raised an eyebrow. "Drinking this." He held up a vial of glowing blue liquid.

"What about me?"

"When you weaken, I will carry you." Trey removed the handcuffs from his side. "Until then, I need you to put these on."

"No." Reece didn't want to be in another bracelet.

Trey shrugged. "Fine, have it your way." He took the opportunity to hit Reece with a glimmering stick.

Reece tried to block the blow, but dizziness made him slip. He grabbed the stick. Trey yanked it from him. It slid through his fingers, taking skin and energy with it.

"What is that?" Reece shook his head to clear his blurred vision. "Is it poisoned?"

Trey didn't answer but hit him on his head, chin, and back. Everywhere the club hit his skin, he felt like it took something with it. Reece felt the energy leave him; with each weakening blow, his hunger raged. He could smell Trey and lunged at him.

Trey held a syringe with glowing blue liquid and stabbed it into Reece's neck mid-air. The agony of the liquid pushed through his veins like a burning needle. Reece's fangs extended, and Trey hit him in the back of the head with a final blow. His eyes blurred, and Reece fell to the floor, face down.

"The necklace Jeb gave you weakens your strength. The poison I filled you with makes you sleep and takes your strength by enhancing the hold of the necklace over you. When you wake up, remember to act human until you need to become the beast you are. Take off that necklace only when the time is right."

"You son of a bi…" Reece was overcome by numbing darkness as the necklace tightened around his throat then twisted to release hooks in his skin. *It burns*.

✧ ✧ ✧

A dungeon? Really, this is what it had come to? He was trapped within his body, and Trey gifted him with another cell. Reece tried to get up, but a thickness pushed down on him, causing him to stumble. Dizziness and nausea assailed his head, but he grunted as he surged up, countering the sensation of pushing against an invisible wall. He reached to his neck to touch the necklace that held his powerful hunger and strength at bay. It was on top of his skin, no longer hidden from himself or those around him. The necklace had a mind of its own, knowing when to reveal itself and when to hide. It connected to his thoughts and reflexes. The necklace responded to his actions before he'd even considered them.

Reece touched it. "What do you give me that keeps me from thirsting?" The need for magic consumption was high, but the desire for blood remained just under the surface. Reece realized he wasn't a typical vampire. Neither was his maker, Zamina. She'd mixed his blood with an ancient Vampire Lord who was used to create her in a lab to become a weapon for the Overlord here in this place they called The Void.

Reece stood and walked to the bars. The Dungeon was carved out of rock walls and had the dampness of a place way underground. He could smell death and sickness heavy in the air. He swallowed down the bile that rose from it. It was an irritating new ability. Reece was still discovering changes within himself. The transformation had only started a few months ago, but it felt like it had been forever.

Rei, he mentally called out to his twin sister. He'd wondered if she could hear him and let him share space in her mind after what he'd done. Nearly killing his twin, his only best friend in the world, made his transformed life even more of a living hell. The guilt was like a heaviness that drenched him in a cloak of aching pain.

"Why me, Zamina? Sometimes...I wish I'd never met you." Reece exhaled. He wrapped his hand around one of the bars.

Rei used to warn him that his vices would get him in big trouble. She was right in more ways than one, and it severed their relationship before what Zamina had done to him destroyed his sister's trust. The bars tingled and crackled, sending a shock that burned him. Reece jerked his hand away and stared at the blackened mark on his tanned palm as the wound slowly weaved its way closed. "I don't want to live forever – like this. The Vigilant Master, Jeb, said that as long as there was a drop of human blood in me, I could be redeemed, that my curse can be a footstool for me to save everyone I love. Why don't I feel like it?"

Reece closed his eyes and lifted his hand to his nose. He smelled of flesh and blood – like a human, but he was a hoax.

Trey wanted him to stay in this cage and wait for what?

He was hungry, and his stomach growled. Reece realized he could stomach food, but the taste was awful. Sadly, the only time he'd enjoyed consuming sustenance was when he'd fed from his sister, his best friend Hook, Megan, and the mermaid. Those were the only times he'd weakened enough to give in to the overwhelming hunger. Maybe, he could be strong enough to make them the only victims of his curse.

Chapter 4

Heeled footsteps sounded in the dank darkness. Because of another enhancement to his body, Reece could see clearly. He squinted hard, wondering if he could push his abilities to see through the thickness of the rock walls. There was depth, but he couldn't see farther without the piercing pain of weakness. He needed to feed on magic or blood to give him the edge to push through the restraint of the necklace. The hunger was dull but still there. The closer the tap of the heels came, the more intoxicating the scent. The essence was different from Trey's, which held a tinge of ash and fire. This scent was sweet and seductive with a chaser of human blood. Reece's mouth watered. He couldn't help it. His fingernails grew, and his incisors itched. He fisted his hands at his sides and held his breath as the last tap from a heeled boot stopped before revealing its owner, who stepped in front of his cell.

Reece remained still, sensing the tiny electric sparks of fear and guilt within the space between them. Why was the person afraid of him? Did Trey give away his secret?

Rapidly, she tapped the floor with her foot. In the darkness of the Dungeon's chamber, he wouldn't have been able to make out the person in front of him. It was a female. A tall one, nearly reaching his nose. She had on a leather cap that fit firmly on her head. Her muted shades sat on her high cheekbones. Through holes in the top of her cap, curly brown hair was pulled up into buns on each side of her head. Wisps of curls escaped the buns, giving her a softer appearance. The rust-colored headpiece matched her vest and softly beaten leather pants that fit snugly over her hips. They were gathered into decorative layers tapered just under her knees on top of her high boots.

She gasped, covering her full lips with her light brown hand. "You? How did you get here? Trey said..."

"You know who brought me here?" Reece didn't want to reveal knowing Trey or how he came to the dungeon. "I was drugged."

"I thought you were destroyed." She stepped closer.

Reece fought the urge to walk toward the bars; he deeply desired to reach out and touch the girl. "Do you know me?" He frowned, studying her closer, deciphering her scent. Then it hit him in the face. It was *familiar*.

She dug a finger under her mask and lifted it. Reece was mesmerized for a moment as she yanked it off, her buns dislodging causing her curls to cascade over her shoulders and down her back.

Her eyes glowed, one auburn, the other blue. The skin around the blue eye was pale white, accented with a white-blonde eyebrow, whereas the other was brandy-brown.

Reece felt intense heat from her gaze, as though his skin would burn if he were closer to her. The angelic light within him rose to the heat and cooled his skin as if battling with the fire from the magic emulating from her eyes. Reece inhaled and knew Ora, Zamina's murderer, stood before him. He growled but braced against the jerk of his body, stopping his lunge forward to attack. The only reason he refrained from attacking was that he needed to keep his head together to make sure his family lived and would be able to get free of this place.

"Hook said he ended you. I couldn't confirm it because I'd been dragged here for questioning." She placed her hands on her hips. "I tried to save you, Reece. I even warned you, but now, if you are here after the way I found you – I know you are like Zamina."

"Not true," his voice ground out. He could never be free after what he'd become, but he owed it to them to sacrifice his life to give them the freedom they deserved.

Her nose wiggled. "You smell human. You even look it. The fact that you haven't transformed to feed off on me is a miracle for a fledgling Vamp-imp."

Reece swallowed, hoping she didn't see the beads of sweat on his forehead. It was almost unbearable not to attack her.

"Ora? What is a Vamp-imp?" He cleared his throat.

"It was what she was created to be. She was a mixed breed, the first success of her kind. The others…they were, well…deformed. Dark grey skin, black eyes, and a hunger for humans. They wouldn't just feed; after dragging their prey into a black ink substance that pooled around them, they consumed them. Vamp-imps can't survive on their own, and many are needed to attack prey and consume. They don't live long, either. But Zamina…she was created. Then she started the virus by attacking one of the shifters

21

guarding her. Her victim turned into a zombie-rabid beast."

"She did that?" Reece exhaled and stepped away from Ora, moving deeper into the cell. "Why did she go to school with innocent people?"

"They said she was cured. The scientists changed her DNA again and had her try to feed off of test subjects. She was never able to turn anyone. Zamina even seemed to lose her desire to feed. That's when they gave me to her to sustain her through my magic."

Reece teased the sharp points of his incisors with the tip of his tongue. Thankfully, they hadn't elongated. The necklace was working, but he still needed to restrain himself. Ora's scent was extremely enticing. "How were you able to do that?"

"It is what I am. An enchanted cursed one. The spawn of a Human and Incubi – known as a Cambion. The only one in existence now." She gathered her hair in her hands and twirled it into a bun. The bun rested at her nape, and she huffed before putting the masked cover back on. "Since the light of my eyes didn't burn you, I know you aren't like Zamina. I never wanted to kill her – she was like a sister to me. It was my job to protect her and protect the humans here. But you…"

"I loved her and couldn't leave her alone."

Ora nodded. "And she loved you, I suppose. I was her only source of sustenance, and for her to pursue you meant she *felt* something, which shouldn't be possible for Vampires or Vamp-imps. They prefer to love their own kind – not their food."

"Was there any other like her?"

"No, I suppose not."

Reece needed to put distance between them to give him some time to process his desire to kill her while desiring to bury his face in her scent, making him want to keep her forever. Savor her like a meal he'd want to consume every day.

He stepped back until his naked chest hit the wall, and he sank down, crossing his legs. "Why are you here?"

"To feed you, clean you up, and take you to the work room."

"I'd rather not go anywhere with you."

"I see." Ora sighed. "Look, Reece, I'm sorry. I never wanted to destroy her – but she made me promise that if it came to that, only I would do it."

"She made you promise to kill her?" he snorted. "Zamina didn't look like she was willing to give in when you attacked her in the cabin."

"Zamina fought because she was protecting you. If she didn't want to die, she would have killed me. She had the power to do so. She pretended to be weak to lure others to her, but Zamina was one of the strongest of her kind – of Vampire-kind actually."

"Did she bite you? Feed from you?"

"No, I was able to contain her hunger with the magic that flows from my body. It's part of my energy, and I can direct it to a source. You are the only one I've seen her feed from, and it scared me."

Blade of Fire

If only you knew fear.

Chapter 5

The tapping of her boot was a needed distraction. Reece's nostrils flared at the scent that filled his cell while she reached into the sack hanging from the belt at her waist. Reece let the aroma tease his nose. Why he didn't get as tempted to taste from Trey, he didn't know. Maybe it was what she was, half-human and half-magical with unique gifts that attracted his darker side. Reece didn't know what his body would do if he got close to her now. His sharp nails were digging into his palms, causing them to bleed. He pressed his fist down into his thigh.

"Thirsty?" She tossed him a small bottle of water. It bounced then rolled, tapping his crossed knee.

Reece snatched it and gulped it down in one swallow. "Hungrier." Maybe eating some food would dim the temptation her magic-laced blood posed for him.

"Oh, I only have snacks." She held out a small ziplocked bag of beef jerky, nuts, cranberries, raisins, and dried bananas. He smelled it, and his stomach coiled at the flat scent.

"Throw it to me?" Reece held up his hand.

"Are you…scared of me?" Ora lowered her head, a small gesture that made Reece wonder why she seemed ashamed.

"Why wouldn't I be? You killed my girlfriend and would have killed me if my best friend didn't tell you he would do it."

She hesitated to hold the bag up high. "I don't expect you to understand what we magicals must do to keep the small population of humans who get lured here safe, but I didn't choose this life. I would never want to kill you or Zamina. I loved her." Tears formed in her eyes, and she let them fall before wiping them away with the back of her hand. "She was the only family I've had for years. You, well…I liked you, but I knew you would be a temptation for Zamina, one that could cost her the only freedom she'd ever had outside of the lab."

"Please throw it to me." Reece cleared his throat. He didn't want to hear her apology. He wanted to punish her, consume her, and end the life she was able to continue by killing Zamina. His anger was there, but in it lay the questions he had about the girl who had infected him with her bites.

She threw it and Reece caught it. He lifted it to his mouth and poured in the contents. Chewing the mixture that tasted like stale crackers, he swallowed, praying it would calm his hunger. Within a few moments, it dulled his urge to crawl to her and bang his body against the bars until he could sink his teeth deep into her neck.

Ora reached behind her, into a leather backpack attached to her vest. "Here are some clothes and shoes that will protect the bottoms of your feet when I take you to the workhouse." She reached through the bars and released them.

Reece watched the items fall to the floor. He waited for the food to settle in his stomach, to satisfy his needs and allow him to pretend to be human. Reece touched his neck where the necklace had settled within his skin. It itched with a heaviness, letting him know it was in control of his strength. He took a few calming breaths before he stood up.

"Do I have to go now? Can it wait?" Reece inhaled slowly, the flavor of her magic in the air teased his tongue. He didn't know how he would react around other magicals. He'd hoped the necklace would completely control his temptation. Apparently, it only kept the edge of it in control.

"No, the Soul Thieves are leaving to hunt the infected shifters. They found a few who got away from the lab when Zamina turned the first group. The infection has left the contained areas and is attacking the shifter packs in the Dead Forest near the High School. It must be cleaned up before the school year starts up again."

"I won't be going back there." Reece snorted. How could he think of starting back at high school when he may not survive past the summer? "Are you?"

"I must go back. I haven't finished my first round of high school. I need to graduate."

"First round?"

"We magicals live a long life and will repeat high school in one lifetime of a human, then again until we begin to appear aged. Some magicals age differently than others, so it really depends."

"Isn't it hard being around people with succubus blood? Aren't you supposed to be a seductress or something?"

"I'm only unable to be around others at certain times of the year. During those times, if I had a mate, we would stay in seclusion. But no one will mate with me. I'm cursed."

Reece walked slowly toward the clothes she'd dropped. He felt her gaze tracking him and the heaviness of desire in it that made him frown. Ora was attracted to him? It must be a side-effect of the vampire transformation his body had undergone. Hypnosis of a victim. He bent to retrieve the clothes and stood. His bare chest felt no temperature, no heat, no cold – just comfort, even though he was still damp from the water. Reece touched his stomach, rubbing it a bit to calm it. He lifted his eyes and caught her staring at him.

"Uh, can you turn around so I can change?"

"Yes, of course." Ora spun as if caught doing something wrong.

Reece grinned. Maybe he could use her interest to his advantage. He took his time changing his clothes and watching her movements to make sure he was right about her attraction.

He noticed she couldn't stop moving. She fought against her desire to turn and see what he was doing.

The pants were snug, definitely out-of-date, and reminded him of a time he would have worn them to spar in his father's gym. They were made of a sturdy fabric that tapered into a snug fit around his ankles. The shoes were flexible like slippers but had a firmer bottom that shaped to the curves of his feet with a silent grip on the ground. The shirt had sleeves and a rounded neck and matched the olive-colored pants. The outfit was comfortable and durable.

Reece closed his eyes briefly and willed his nails to retract. Taking a glance down at himself, and adding several calming breaths, he relaxed. "I'm done changing."

Ora slowly pivoted; a smile bloomed on her face. "You look like the others. I can sneak you in now." Her hands had started to glow, and she enclosed one of them around one of the bars. Several of the bars moved in sync, sliding to create an opening he could walk through.

Reece stepped through and smoothly stood next to Ora. Close, maybe a bit too close, but he had to take just one more sniff before he'd tamp down the beast within.

"Are you sure you're alright?"

Reece swallowed. "I'm okay...the drug, maybe it had some long-term effects."

She frowned. "Maybe... Your eyes, they're changing colors from the brown I remember."

"My eyes are hazel." At least when he was a baby, but they'd turned brown until Zamina's infection took over.

"Good." She snapped a handcuff onto his wrist.

"What's this for?" Reece tugged at the binding and dropped his shoulders, relieved she believed his explanation. He felt he could break them but didn't want to give himself away. He dropped his hands in front of him, feigning resignation.

"That's to make sure you don't try to escape. The workhouse is where you have to prove your worth or die. If you show a special skill, the Overlord may call you to his court to create something especially for him. That will move you to his wing. That is where you need to be."

29

"Have you been there?"

"No. I am not allowed. He doesn't like females who have the power to seduce around him. I've only been managed by his second in command, and she is awful."

Reece walked slightly behind her, allowing his wrists to remain slack so he was easily led through the dark dungeon. The floor was broken and ragged. The cells were sparsely scattered between protruding rocks. The other cells seemed vacant, and only the stale smell of wet rock lingered around the path.

"He—"

"She is strange. It's rumored she is from the realm of Demi-gods and has snakes for hair, although she keeps a wrap over it, so no one knows. She also covers her eyes with dark glasses. All I know is I feel uncomfortable when I'm called to answer her demands."

Demi-gods? Reece didn't want to think about meeting the woman either. All he wanted was to get close enough to the Overlord to find a weakness. Then locate the entrance Zamina found out of this place.

"Why aren't other prisoners here?"

"This dungeon is closed. It's where the rabid shifters, who lived here on the grounds, were found. No magical or Soul Warrior wants to come here. It was rumored a few stray ones got loose in the Dungeon. Since it's far from the main castle, they torched the place, and no one has been to clean it since."

"Who torched it?"

"Trey's team. It's why he put you here."

30

"How do you know him?"

"Jeb."

Chapter 6

Reece wondered if Ora was a Vigilant. She'd hardly spoken to him when he was with Zamina. All she did was warn him against being with Zamina as if Reece could've stopped himself from wanting a vampire — vamp-imp.

He was working for Jeb, who had to know Ora had killed his girlfriend. Though Ora's story seemed believable, the tears in her eyes when mentioning Zamina were real — Reece still wanted to punish her for taking away his lover. Why did she have to destroy Zamina in such a brutal death?

At least for now, his body was sated. He still hungered for the magic with her blood as a chaser, but not to the point of losing control. The necklace had done its job — for now.

She led him through the abandoned dungeon that appeared dug out of the rock. He thought it was built on an incline since each step seemed to be on an elevated rock pathway. Cells—dug out of the rock, lined each side, no windows, thick bars, and uneven rock floor—were identical in size. The stench of animals, death, and sickness hung in the air behind the stench of thick smoked ash.

Ahead, a pale light filtered in, and Reece stopped to look out of the barred window. The moon was high and dim. He walked over to it, letting Ora's heels echo ahead of him. He peered out at the grey moon. Beneath them, dusky clouds. Below that thick mist.

"Don't think about going out there. The mist will eat you. It's not mist but lurking sentinels of Kelpies. They protect this side of the Overlord's castle in case the rabbit shifters try to return. The Kelpies hang out in the elements in wait. The cousins of the Kelpies, though, are always moving and don't like to gather as much."

Reece focused on movement in the fog lake that hugged the building and swore he captured a female lying in the mist as if napping.

"It's not what you think. They will give you an allusion to lure you closer."

He nodded. "What will I see when I get to the workroom?"

"Nothing. I am sneaking you in while the others are working the lava lake. You won't be considered a prisoner, only someone we found by mistake."

"No one will wonder?"

"I can make it so they don't question the assumption."

Reece narrowed his gaze at Ora. Her powers were strong. Interesting, but he would let her reveal her unique abilities. She seemed to talk more when he kept quiet. A nervous behavior he hadn't seen in her before when they'd met.

"How do you know your way around here?"

She shrugged. "It's one of my abilities. I can capture

clues from magical residue. Some hold memories of their owner or magical talents I can mimic. Not many know about this quality of my being."

"Why would you tell me?"

"My honesty is my only penance. I have nothing else to give." She turned to him. "I told you; I am sorry about Zamina. I can only hope that you can forgive me and understand why I had to do what was done."

Reece didn't respond. Forgiveness for murder? He'd have to work on that because, honestly, he had no right to be angry with Ora. Reece would have killed his twin sister if she hadn't had the strength born of an angel to fight him off. If he were honest, his mother would have met an end the many times he'd tested his power to restrain himself from seeking others to feed on. Even so, he didn't have it in him to move in the direction of forgiveness. He needed to just do what he came to do, and maybe he would ask Ora to do him the same favor she did for Zamina. End his torture. Would his family forgive him? His carelessness, desire, and stupidity could have killed them all because of his hunger. Jeb helped him to control his nature and gave him hope.

"Let's go."

Her eyes fell to the floor, and she inhaled then turned to lead the way again.

Reece felt her sadness. How was that possible? The only emotions he'd been able to physically sense were his twin sister's. Though, when he turned vamp-imp and angel, he stayed far away from anyone. It was hard to tell what he was capable of sensing.

35

The slanted floor with its protruding rocks scattered within the ash didn't make it a comfortable path, but Reece silently followed Ora to the steep stairwell, issuing a dim gray glow from the moon teasing the top of the clouds.

"The cuffs?" Reece tugged on them.

She smirked. "You can climb the stairs with them on."

He shrugged. "I don't know. We *humans* are fragile."

She stepped closer. "Can I trust you? As one Vigilant to another?"

"For that, yes."

So, she knew he was working with Jeb. Being a Vigilant was confusing, and he'd only done it because he had no other choice. He needed forgiveness from someone, and the Vigilants' creator were granting it. He thought by accepting the call of the Most High and the order of Melchizedek, he would be saved. Freed from his cursed affliction – but instead, he had to live with his struggle. The affliction had stuck around. At least, now he wasn't alone in it.

"Don't test me. What we are here to accomplish is much larger than what is between us."

"There is no us. Only saving my family. And maybe a small favor I'd ask of you for killing my girlfriend."

Ora flinched. "Fine. Don't make me regret this."

I've only begun to serve you regrets.

Chapter 7

They were outside. The air was heavy and oppressive with moisture. Dark shrubs and trees covered the black grass beneath their feet. The sky was grey with the backdrop of black trees on gray trunks. The dungeon appeared safer than the thick wood and brush surrounding them.

"I hear water," Reece stated.

"There is a moat around most of the grounds I've seen so far. No one can survive it. There are creatures within it that counter the energy from magic. The Overlord controls them. These woods—" She gestured with a slight tilt of her head— "lead to the workhouse. I will conceal us."

Ora raised her hands and then snapped her arms out at the elbow. A black orb descended on them as they walked.

"What is that?"

"I gathered the dark matter and reflected it against the light. Nothing magical can see beyond this since it's like cutting through the fabric of the atmosphere."

"Whoa! How'd you know you could do that?"

"I did it the first time I experienced grief when they killed my father, who was trying to protect me from being captured."

"You didn't get away?"

"No. It didn't last long, and I was too young to understand what I had done."

"Is that how you appeared out of nowhere when you attacked Zamina?"

"Yes. Now be quiet; we are almost there. I want to get us to our location before others come to get in the way."

Reece followed while glancing at the black leaves and charred trunks that seemed to seep an oily substance from their bodies. One of the trees moved as if it sensed something or someone moving around it. They'd traveled several yards, and a tall structure with smoke emitting from its chimney came into view. It was grey with sharp square angles and small boxy windows. The white door was slightly ajar and was tremendous at twenty feet tall.

"What's with the large doors?"

"For the giants, large magicals, and Berserkers who guard the outer perimeter and portals to the Realms."

"Realms?"

"There are many. They're all controlled by the Overlord. The Fae Realm, the Vampire Realm, the Trickster Realm, and the Ancient Realm. The Void stands between them and the Earth Realm."

Reece would have thought her crazy and delusional if she'd told him this before he became a monster. After that experience, there was not much he wouldn't believe possible.

They pivoted their bodies and slid through the crack in the doors. Reece's eyes widened. The workhouse had high ceilings and a lot of open space. There was a wall of stone in the back with another separating wall of thick gray bricks. Between the structure and brick walls was a tunnel with a glowing green light that seemed to pulse within. From the ceilings, there were chains that pulled down shelves with levers for ladders that led up to various tools. The ceiling had several large, square multi-colored tiles in different states of use. Each ceiling block could be pulled down to reveal a tool used in creating various weapons, devices, or manipulating stone. Some of the ceiling tiles were lowered to the floor in suspended shelves with glowing floating orbs or tools, and some held jars of imprisoned Faeries with labels for the type of magical dust they produced. Others were firmly attached to the ceiling, and he could see their access from a long chain sticking out from its corner. The floor was of rock that had veins of some green illuminating substance moving through it in rippling waves. Long tables with no order or direction were created of rock or crystallized stones. The chairs were made of wood, but not sanded or smooth. They bore the shapes of the trees they'd been cut from with twigs of green or brown sticking out here and there.

Reece walked over to the metalwork section where various ovens were heated and ready. Inside each were bright orange coals. The place appeared as though people had been working but had been stopped abruptly.

"This is like nothing I've seen." He spun around.

"You can fit in. Hide until they return. You can slip in during the chaos and then get to work to create something that will impress the Overlord. I am one of the guards here and will create a story about how you arrived. The others will have passage out by the Mist Ones; you will have to come with me when night falls."

Reece raised an eyebrow. With so many magicals around, he wondered how he could keep the taunting hunger at bay. His tongue pushed against his teeth as if it had a mind of its own at the direction of his thoughts. He spied a door next to the ovens.

"Is it safe to go in here?" Reece pointed.

"Oh yes. That's one of the supply closets for tools. Hurry, I hear them."

Reece quickly opened the door and slid into the dark room. He turned on the lights as the murmurs from outside the door gradually got louder. The scent hit him then, so deliciously addictive his knees buckled. He'd become a fiend and couldn't help but inhale, taking in the unchecked magical energy that sifted through the door's crack. His tongue licked his lips, and he opened his mouth to slowly draw more of it inside his hiding place. Like a rainbow of glitter, unchecked magic floated into his opened mouth.

"I'm tired all of a sudden," someone murmured.

Another laughed. "You're always tired."

Reece closed his eyes briefly; sated from the taste and draw of the magic he'd consumed. Having a chaser of blood would be so satisfying, but, after nearly killing his sister on his first feed, he'd vowed to never draw blood from another.

He smelled her then. His enemy and ally, Ora was standing next to the door. Reece straightened and bent his shoulders a bit to appear meek and not strengthened by his consumed nourishment.

Ora gave a hand signal. He knew it was a clue that it was clear for him to come out to mingle with the crowd. Reece slipped out of hiding. He sauntered over to one of the long metal tables containing discarded tools, broken rocks, and other cast-off equipment. His eyes landed on a hammer, and he picked it up.

"That's mine," a deep voice stated behind him.

Reece didn't move right away. Whoever had spoken was taller than him, which wasn't typical. He lifted the heavy flat-sided hammer and pivoted. He forced his eyes not to widen at the male holding out his hand, waiting for the tool. His skin was orange. Veins of glowing magic protruded from his forehead, cheekbones, and chin in an artful design with a flow of bright magic that pulsed within them. Reece dropped the hammer into his hand.

The magical pivoted away. Reece realized he was in a sea of creatures he'd only read about. Nymphs, satyrs, and elven creatures worked on tools for war. Weapons and designs beyond what Reece had read about or studied in history.

A girl in a tight leather vest, her cream shirt spilling over the top, with long blonde hair to her hips, tsked at him. "Lazy ones don't get paid, you know?"

Reece smelled the dew of the morning and the wood from the trees on her skin and reflected in her green eyes. "I'm not lazy, just thinking."

"Don't think too long. That guard over there will send

you with the mist that can eat you instead of taking you home."

He knew without looking she was talking about Ora. Reece felt the daggers from her gaze tickle his back. "Excuse me, I need to get back to work." He wanted to avoid the distraction of another meal to sway him from finding something like the rare metal he'd once used to make his dagger.

After spending a few more moments at the table, Reece moved to the corner of the room where the ovens stood. The bladesmiths were working in unison on several swords. Most of the magicals working looked similar, tall and thick with glowing white eyes set in dark smooth skin. Their arms were protected by wide sleeves that flowed easily with each movement.

Reece gathered discarded materials and scraps, found a clear space, and started to work with those pieces. *Become invisible.* He needed to be left alone until he could find a way to the secret passage to the garden where Zamina escaped to see him. The sooner he found it, the closer he'd be to becoming free of Megan's death bargain.

Chapter 8

Reece was focused on hammering his frustrations while he waited for the right moment to slip out of the workhouse. Magicals were elitist. They ignored him, grunted at him, or pointed. Apparently, they considered him weak. That was perfect and, in the end, would give him the edge he needed. He had to wait to get to the main castle. He'd heard a nymph mention it being where the Overlord resided. Zamina's adopted brother's home was the key to the mystery Reece needed.

We need to leave before the mist comes to collect the workers. Ora's voice echoed in his mind. Reece forced down the urge to push her out. His ability to do so had strengthened with his transformation, and he didn't want to give her a clue about his abilities.

"How?" Reece pivoted around and frowned at her, wondering how her voice was in his head. The only other person to do that to him was his sister.

"You!" Ora grabbed his arm. "Gather the scraps off the ground and put them in the wheelbarrow."

Reece smirked. So, they were playing the bad cop game now. He'd bite. Without saying a word, he stopped hammering and retrieved the wheelbarrow propped up against the wall next to the fire pit. No one paid him much attention. They'd likely been used to seeing the guards bark out demands. The wheelbarrow was worn but sturdy. Reece maneuvered it around one beastly magical or another, picking up scraps of wood, metal, and shards of crystals off the ground.

Someone snickered. "A human? What is it doing here?"

He smirked. They'd be chasing him down if they only knew what he truly was.

Reece kept his chin lowered, trying to appear weak and submissive, but the power from the magic he'd consumed while hiding in the closet like a drug fiend drummed through his blood. Even so, it felt muted, like something was holding the burst of power with it at bay. Could it be the necklace had sunken into his skin to conceal its hold on him? Ora walked with her back straight in a commanding tone that belied her delicate beauty. He wanted to taste her magic again; it was unlike the others. His incisors shifted, piercing his tongue with their sharpness as he imagined sinking them into her neck. He closed his eyes for a moment to push down the taunting thought.

Ora led him out the doors. It was dark with a yellow moon that cast a muted glow. Instead of going back in the direction of the black forest, they made a turn down a rock-paved walkway leading away from the workhouse. They walked toward a bridge that disappeared into the thick fog.

"I found someone to take us to the Overlord's castle."

Reece released the handles of the wheelbarrow. "How?"

"I am gifting him with a sword made for me. He can

become an ally. Besides, that sword…I can't keep it, and I won't give it to the Overlord."

"Okay, so we wait here?"

The mist formed into the face of a man with a round head, long chin, and thick arms with chains on them, reminding Reece of a Genie. His skin was green, and his eyes were brown.

"You finally arrived. My time is limited. Did you put the exchange item where I told you to?"

"Yes, it's in the dungeons, hidden in one of the cells in the back."

"Good, good. Now we must hurry before my sisters of the mist and brothers realize I am not with them to pick up the magical craftsmen."

The man in the fog's face lost its color and shape.

"Come, we have to hold each other so he takes us as one."

Reece raised an eyebrow. "You trying to cop a feel from your prisoner?"

"No! Hurry." She stomped her feet.

Reece moved close to Ora. He refused to let her hold him like he was a weakling. Besides, if he pulled her close, he'd be able to sneak a bit of her magic. He grabbed her wrist and tugged her into his arms. Her eyes widened in confusion. He tucked her head into his chest as the fog surrounded them. It was wet and suffocating. With each moment that passed by, he grew colder until the pressure was almost freezing. Ora's arms tightened around him. Reece dipped his nose into her hair. The sweet nectar of her mix of magic and human tickled his nose. He opened his mouth to inhale. Reece's incisors lengthened. Saliva dripped, and he lowered his head to lick it from the side of her face, stealing just a small taste of her essence. She sighed in his arms, and, for a moment, he had the strongest desire to kiss Ora. He didn't want to do that to any of his other prey. He didn't feel comfortable with the sensation and pushed her away from him a bit. The fog around them swirled as if they were in the center of a tornado until it dissipated into thin air with them.

He'd blanked out. Reece blinked, disorientated. Ora pushed off his chest. He ignored her reaction and looked around to see where the magical had put them.

Chapter 9

It's a safe place. Hidden from the Soul Warriors. The Overlord's plan is not a good one for any of us. I trust this trade will not fail," said the man with green skin, firm muscled arms exposed. He was adorned in a richly ornate vest resting on top of pants that ballooned out. The pants tapered to shoes of gold embellished with crystals.

"I made you a promise. The sword is powerful enough to cut through anything – even crystals of magic." Ora stood up straight.

Reece watched the exchange.

The magical glanced at Reece. "You trust this human can survive the Overlord's scrutiny?"

"He created the sword. His talent will be of use to the Overlord's purpose. The magic within the sword must accept the shaping from its handler. Reece has proven himself worthy to create the weapon the Overlord wants. You have the sword. The Overlord will have the maker."

"Very well. I will use it to free my love and will not remain to help you until I can be sure of her safety. The Mist Ones and Kelpie are easily persuaded to work against the Overlord's wishes by refusing to disburse the Soul Warriors to their stations in light of an attack. You will have to find someone you can trust to lure them away. My people can be fickle and are primed for tipping the scales for their freedom. Don't make me regret this, but finish what you started."

Ora nodded. "I will."

"To leave here, go through the tunnels. The Soul Warriors rarely check them. The West Wing was where the girl Zamina lived. That wing has been shut down since she was put down. I don't know why they allowed her kind to live amongst the magicals. The sickness continues, and I am told it spread to the outer regions of The Void. It is possibly making its way to where Newputton is, and the humans there will surely have to be protected."

"Where do the tunnels lead?"

"To the Relic wing. He can start working there unnoticed. If he can create something impressive, present it to the Soul Thief who guards there. He is sympathetic to our cause. But don't trust him with anything else."

"Thank you."

"I must go before my use of my magic is detected." The man waved his hand and returned to a body of thick fog. The fog disappeared, and Ora turned to Reece.

"What did I just see?"

"You met Sahazzar, an Ashta. He is the leader of the Kelpie and Mist creatures. Ashta is the ancient line of Genies who control their own magic for their realm. The Overlord stripped him of his position and forced him into hiding when he spoke against the war. He would have escaped here, but until he turns himself in to be destroyed, he is trying to free his wife, whom the Overlord has imprisoned."

Reece looked around the room and realized it held no furniture. No bed or chairs, just lights embedded into the smooth walls resembling cement. The door was metal, flat, with a grey handle. He grasped it and pushed down. The door opened to reveal a tunnel. It had the same precise, smooth, angular walls as the room, but there was no light. He blinked and could clearly see the path to his right but turned to the left and realized it was a dead end.

"There is no light in the tunnel." Reece made sure to leave the door slightly ajar. It would make his escape easier later.

Ora shrugged. "I can see in the dark. You will have to stay close to me."

Close to her, Reece thinned his lips. He wasn't hungry any longer. Thanks to their first stop, he'd sated himself. Hopefully, his binging on magic and salivating for blood wouldn't return for some time.

"We should rest while we can." Ora walked to a corner.

Reece surmised she wanted distance. He wasn't willing to give it to her, not that easily. "It's cold in here. Are you uncomfortable?" He fisted his hands at his sides. "Do you mind if we sit next to each other?"

She sighed. "I don't know if I should trust you that much. You did say once that you would kill me."

"I said that in anger and fear. I'm no longer scared of you."

Ora laughed. "You should be. I could break your human body with my bare hands. I could seduce you then stab you through your heart with my nails. Don't see my human body and think I am not magical."

"I don't doubt you. I can't apologize for the way I felt because, at the time, and after what I witnessed, those feelings were real. I loved her – or who I wanted to believe she was – and she was the first girl I'd felt that stirring with. You killed her. I wanted to kill you. Now, I'm not so sure."

"So, are you apologizing for saying you would kill me? That you hated me?" Ora frowned, studying Reece intently.

He knew she was looking for clues, thinking he was a liar. "I am saying I don't feel that way anymore. I understand why you did it. She could have killed me, infected me with some zombie virus, or changed me into what she was – or something else."

"And you are sure nothing happened to you when you left? Hook was supposed to destroy you if you'd been changed."

"Hook would have killed me where I stood if he smelled a change in me."

Ora raised an eyebrow. "You knew he was a werewolf?"

Reece chuckled. "Yeah, he convinced me to set up some frat football guys who were vandalizing my cars and his house. Things got weird, and I knew he was different." Reece didn't want to tell her the entire truth, that he'd fed off Hook's blood until Jeb found a way to control his magic and bloodlust. Reece would reveal this truth when it was time – when he would ask Ora to put him out of his misery as she did Zamina.

"He must have trusted you not to hide it."

"I trusted him. He saved my life by introducing me to Jeb."

She frowned. "You knew Jeb well?"

"I did. He gave me the materials to create the sword you used to murder Zamina." Reece thinned his lips.

Ora flinched. "Oh, he charged me a hefty price for it. I bought it to kill the Overlord, not for Zamina."

"Why didn't you kill the Overlord with it?"

"I couldn't get close enough to him and didn't trust anyone in his presence to do it for me. It was the price I paid to Jeb. I wanted to stop Cyrillus from storming the veil to the Earthen realm."

"I know you will do it. You are good at murder."

Ora blinked several times as if fighting against a response to his jab. "I am not. I don't like it, but I was trained as security, protector, and warrior. I have avoided having to kill and even fought for Zamina to survive when she caused the first outbreak. Sometimes, to survive and to save others from themselves, we must do what we are forced to do. Tell me, would you have killed her to protect your family if you knew what she was?"

Reece wiped a hand down his face, thinking about it. Knowing what he knew, yes, he would have killed Zamina if she'd shown herself as a vampire. He didn't want to say the words out loud to admit his duality – his hypocrisy.

"Humph." Her gaze seemed to assess what his mouth couldn't admit. "Are you hungry? I got us some food." Ora slid her leather belt around; it had a small sack hooked on it. "Some dried jerky, peanuts, and dried fruit. Only this small bottled water was left."

"I'm good. You can have it."

"Alright." Ora went to the corner and sat cross-legged. "You can sit next to me."

Reece slowly walked over, enjoying the scent of her magical essence that filled the room. He sat beside her and crossed his legs.

"The sword—the one you got from Jeb—can you tell me about the metal it's made from?"

"The metal is from a sacred place. The place where the Overlord got his stolen magic. He killed the guardians when he stole it. If his late wife hadn't followed him and fought him over the crystal, he would have been powerful enough to take over the Earth realm. If she hadn't stopped him and broken the crystal, she wouldn't have become the veil of extra protection between the Realms. He couldn't break through it. The Vigilant has since tried to find a way to remove the crystal from him, but he is the only one known to be powerful enough to withstand the consuming fire that is a side effect of the stone."

"He killed a Vigilant to get to the crystal?"

"Yes, and one of their most powerful warriors. Ever since, they've been trying to retrieve the crystal and return, but none of them is strong enough to fight the army of the Overlords, much less fight him. So, they wait."

"Hmmm? What about Megan? Is she powerful enough to take it?"

Ora laughed. "If she was, who can trust her to wield the power for anyone but herself?"

"True, Megan only cares about her own agenda."

Reece leaned closer to Ora. He needed her trust and maybe even a brief friendship for now. He closed his eyes and hoped his family had gotten free even if he never would be.

I'm sorry, Reece. He felt a light touch on his hair. Ora had just become a bit more complicated. He responded to her plea. *Sleep, Ora, sleep.*

He held her apology in his mind. It made his heart pump, knowing she was remorseful. Reece needed her to go into a deep sleep so he could bring this nightmare of his life to rights. Part of him was starting to care for Ora, and he didn't need that. Not now, not ever. He knew he was a monster and would consume her the moment she allowed him to taste her blood-laced magic. Unfortunately for her, it was all he could think about.

Chapter 10

Reece slowly moved Ora's head, which was tucked between his shoulder and his ear. Finally, he felt her body slump into a deep sleep. He slid down to rest on the corner wall next to her. He had to find the wing where Zamina stayed. Reece was sure it would reveal the hidden exit to the castle that he could open for the Vigilant to attack. He vaguely remembered Zamina telling him about a painting of the donor for her creation. She'd found the entrance to the garden through a hidden passage behind the frame.

Reece slid out of the door. The comfortable clothes she'd given him made for a quiet exit. He jogged the remainder of the distance. Thin flaps slid in front of his pupils as his hunting instinct took over, and he followed a tiny mouse with his eyes. The creature had scurried into a crack in the wall, sensing it had a predator in its midst. Reece smiled. He didn't blame the rodent.

The tunnel came to an end at a tall wooden door. He slid it aside and realized he was in some storage room. The drop from the door was about six feet, a decent fall if you weren't watching your step.

Jumping down, he looked back up and realized the door was painted like the rest of the wallpaper covering the room.

The designs were of meadows of yellow and orange flowers on a muted cream-colored background. It was hideous, but Reece figured it did a good job of hiding the secret entrance. The room was packed with dust, as though it hadn't been entered in years. Small footprints on the path between leaning wood shelves filled with what Reece eyed as artful pots, vases, and antiques were covered in spider webs, dust, and the heavy scent of mildew. He didn't like how acute his sense of smell had become. Part of his stomach recoiled from the aromas that were once dulled by his human senses. The room was forgotten, and Reece hoped the area outside of it was as well.

He opened the tall wood-planked door. It was sturdy and thick and squeaked from neglect as he pushed it. The long walkway was devoid of movement, with scattered statues of gold and silver and uniquely chiseled art within the walls. One was of a giant woman with the pointed ears of a Fae. The other was of a Berserker poised for attack, club held high to pound on scattering humans running from the attack. Reece tried not to become absorbed in the art carved in the walls of the hallway, but even though they were dusted over with blotches of webs, they were captivating.

The end of the hall was only a few steps away. Reece hesitated at the echo of voices in the distance. Making sure his steps were silent, he put his back to the wall and waited for them to fade. He counted a few moments, and the silence was consistent.

Reece stepped around the curve. The hall opened into a rounded atrium. Moonlight spilled through the ceiling in an orange glow, onto a podium with a marble globe. The globe was black, seemingly void of engravings; except when the orange light from the moon touched it, the globe's hidden engravings illuminated. The words were not in a language he could understand, but the pictures were evidently a map of the palace and its surrounding grounds. Reece touched the globe, moving it back and forth with his fingers, closing his eyes briefly to solidify the paths in his brain. Being a racecar driver, he had to be a quick study of maps to plan his path to victory. Now would be no different. He would win, and the revenge he would rain on Megan would be worth it.

A scent tickled his nose, causing him to glance around the open atrium. Someone was near; he sensed it. Even though the voices had moved on, Reece felt as though he wasn't alone. That he was being observed. There was nothing in the atrium, so he shrugged and took the hall to the left, knowing from the map that the two other exits from the atrium were to wings of the castle used for housing supplies, artifacts, and energy-producing filtration systems. Even though these magicals could control the elements, they still relied on technology and science to survive.

The new hallway teemed with the artwork. It was strange, dark art with paintings of different mystical creatures in all forms of imprisonment. It was hard to look at for long as the beings within them seemed to have eyes that cried out for help.

His footsteps were silent. He knew he'd have to be careful as he came to the end of the hall. It led to a breezeway path to the back of the castle kitchens. He had to get close to the metalworks and weapons wing. There, he could create a weapon, something to carry that wouldn't reveal his abilities. Even though he didn't know all of his abilities, he noticed that his body now worked on instinct. Primal, animal, and it took over control of his usually methodical thinking.

Chapter 11

His head snapped up; the smell of the sea, salt, and female tickled his nostrils. A thin mist snaked above him on the tall gray ceiling of the castle's dark hall. He saw it, flat, tracking and hesitating as if assessing him. He waited for it to form as it decided to confront him. Reece didn't want to leave bodies or missing magicals around before he could earn their trust, learn their secrets, and keep them imprisoned in this Void they called home.

In a flash, the mist thickened, poured to the floor ahead of him, and shaped itself into a beautiful woman. Her pale skin was adorned in a gold bodice that covered her breasts while teardrop emeralds hung from it, falling onto her exposed stomach. Her sheer-white pants flared out then tapered at the ankles in a green and gold decorated loop that fits around her middle toe. Her stormy gray eyes nailed him.

"What are you doing here?" She pointed. Her long golden hair was pulled up to the top of her head, adorned in a jeweled hoop around a thick braid.

"I am lost, actually." He wasn't lying. Reece smiled. "I was dropped off but was left in a hurry. They may have mistakenly delivered me to the wrong place."

Her eyes narrowed. "Where are you to go?"

"I am a swordsmith. One of the best of my kind." Reece didn't want to tell what he was; he wanted her to guess. It would let him know what these magicals assumed he was, and he would play to that.

"Humans? Are they letting you within these walls? The Overlord must be desperate."

Reece shrugged. "My talent speaks for itself."

She came close, her steps silent but firm on the smooth rock floor of the hall. "You are the first human I've seen in…a long time."

"You are like what we would call a Genie. Do you come in a bottle? Grant wishes?"

"Those are my sisters." She laughed. "They have been captured by human wizards who come here to steal our magic – our knowledge. I would never let them catch me. Those are slaves to the human offspring of Merlin and the like. I will never be a slave to a human."

Reece raised an eyebrow. "But you are the Overlord's slave?"

She reached out and touched his hair. "No, I am in his army. I choose to be here. But he does have a certain hold on my people." The magical stepped closer, standing on her tiptoes to sniff his neck. "You look human, but something about you smells different."

"I really need to get to the Relic wing. There is little time for me to pay my debt and create something the Overlord can use. Something to impress him."

She stepped back and said, "I will take you there myself," and then smiled.

Reece felt her inner struggle and saw it in her grey eyes that seemed to hold a storm within them. "Thanks. Do you think we can walk there? I got sick the last time I was transported." Reece teased at his desire to persuade her to do his will. It was testing. Where her magic was visible, his abilities seemed to go undetected by others. He saw the invisible hand that snaked out from him to touch her head.

"Walk? That is not the way subjects move about here. You need to allow me to take you into the mist to get to that location. It's the way things are done here."

"Can I at least know your name?" Reece smiled. He smelled the magic on her and, for a moment, had to hold back his instinct to feed.

She laughed. "DewOfWinter, and you?"

"I don't know my name. I had a bad accident." Reece would need a new name, something to acknowledge what he had become. He hadn't thought about it before, but he didn't feel like a Reece any longer.

"Hmmm, typical. You humans are not very strong. Being exposed to magicals has caused many to faint or die on the spot."

"I can imagine," Reece responded flatly, not wanting to give her any indication that she had underestimated his abilities. Within seconds, her expression changed from one of disdain to complicity. He pushed his will, his thoughts, into hers. *You will take me to the wing of weapons and respond to my call whenever I need you.*

"Come closer," she whispered. The image of her body thinned to a translucent image, and a gray smokey mist rose around Reece.

"Are you a Genie? Have you been to my home?"

The female stomped. "I am not enslaved and bound to the Earth realm like my people tricked into going there by the wizard Merlin for amusement. I have never, nor will ever, want to go to your home."

She smelled divine. He couldn't help but lick at her magic essence. He felt the thick mist rise into a cocoon of a tornado, and he shivered a bit. Her scent surrounded him, lulled him into deep fatigue, and within moments, Reece was lifted into a space where his body and mind seemed to be separated, weightless. Part of him wanted to grab the broken particles of himself that floated away.

What had she done to him?

Chapter 12

His throat was dry, and his neck was stiff. Reece struggled to open his eyes. DewOfWinter stood above him with her arms crossed.

"What did you do to me, human?" She frowned.

"I don't know what you mean." Reece recovered and jumped off the floor, not wanting to be vulnerable. His strength returned, and his mind's sharpness was on alert.

"I had no intention of bringing you here, yet here we are."

Reece wanted to look around but didn't give in to it. He made sure he kept his eyes on DewOfWinter.

"Where were you taking me?" Reece forced his stance to be comforting, weak, and respectful of her magic.

"I was going to consume you, but I couldn't. I needed to bring you here."

"Maybe that is the protection spell used to, uh, keep me safe until I finish what I was sent here to do."

"Perhaps." She crossed her arms. "The others aren't here yet. The Soul Warriors will be coming into this wing soon. Be careful of them. They may be human, but they are infused with magic and dislike for their own kind."

DewOfWinter bit her lip then covered her mouth with her hand.

"I've heard." Reece cleared his throat. "And thank you for not eating me."

She swallowed, eyeing him suspiciously. "I won't eat you. But my sisters may. I like to drown my victims then give their parts for trade." She laughed, turned into a thick gray blob, and then disappeared.

Dropping his shoulders, he glanced at the high ceiling darkened by soot from the fires used to make the weapons. Reece slowly pivoted and was impressed by the size of the wing-turned-workroom. It was larger than the workhouse he'd gone into earlier. Metal shelves in rows on the left lined the walls. The shelves went from floor to ceiling and had a rolling ladder on each of the four long rows of supplies. Light beamed down on them, casting a golden glow onto the tops of the shelves, which held large broken pieces of gems, crystals, and diamonds of many colors. Reece could smell the energy encased within them. All were in different flavors of the same scent.

He stepped over to the cleared portion of the room where three massive rock ovens were chiseled into the wall. They held calm ambers of illuminating rocks with sprinkles of flames dancing on the rocks within them. Tools hung on a wall near the long metal worktables that had chairs of all sizes scattered around them. Some chairs were tall enough for a giant while others were smaller, like for dwarfs, with still-smaller tables that could be pulled out from beneath the larger one for those creatures. Electrical tools with no cords to plug them in were in the other corner. Reece wondered how those were started. Magic or technology?

He turned from the ovens and went to the shelves. He took his time doing an inventory of what was on which shelf. It was tedious, but going up and down the ladder through the four rows allowed him time to think and plan what he would create. A Katana teased his creative mind, or maybe he could design a Roman Gladius for their sleekness and craftmanship. All he needed was there and more. Some of the chipped crystals could be placed into the handle, and maybe if he could find that subtle yet powerful metal Jeb had given him, he could create something even more unique.

Voices floated above the air, teasing Reece's sensitive hearing. He jumped down from the ladder he was on. The shelf in front of him had long metal pieces of various thicknesses stacked on it. He grabbed a piece of scrap metal off the shelf along with a bag sitting next to it. Reece hurried to the nearest table and drew the metal pieces out of the bag slowly while keeping his eyes on the door. It opened without resistance with a loud groan. Men and women, some who even seemed to be teenagers, came into the room. They had on dark outfits with black vests bearing a symbol on them. All were dressed similarly, and all were human, but the soot of hell showed within their skin. Their diversity in age, color, and height made them capable of infiltration into many places in the fake Newport, RI town Reece had thought they lived in. He could swear some of them were teachers and students at the high school he attended. Soul Warriors, where the males were called Soul Thieves and the females were Soul Trainers.

"You! How'd you get here?"

Reece dropped his head. Then he jerked it up, making sure to open his eyes with surprise and a bit of fear. "I, uh, the mist brought me here."

A ruddy-haired guy stormed over to him. He was tall, but Reece looked at him nearly eye to eye. "The stupid smoke people dropped off a human." The guy leaned in, his eyes narrowing at Reece, then sniffed him. "Yeah, human alright. He's practically shivering."

"I… don't know why I am here. She said to make weapons." Reece dropped his hands beneath the table, balling his fists against the scent of these Soul Warriors. They smelled human but with a heavy stink of dark magic and an underlying tinge of soot from ashes. The draw to feed from them was there, but something in him was repulsed by the remnants of hellfire that hung on them. Reece swallowed down the bile that rose in him and stepped back.

One of the older females approached the big guy and put a hand on his shoulder. "The mist has their orders, and we have ours. Let him work. Others will arrive to prove themselves to the Overlord. If he is not worthy, the mist will return him back – with no memory of being here."

Reece turned away from them and continued to work. Magicals appeared in a whirl of smokey mist with various male and female mist creatures dressed like Genies: a troll, an ogre, shifters, and a few Centaurs.

"Get to work! You only have until nightfall to present your best work. Those who present something worthy will stay, those who don't – go with the mist."

Reece thought hard; he needed to get close to the Overlord, but he wanted to find the wing that led to the gardens. He smiled, thinking of DewOfWinter, and wondered if his abilities would allow him to call her to him once again.

He shrugged at the grumbling from the other captives around him and picked up a hammer. Time to let them see his true talent.

Chapter 13

N ot worthy." The older Soul Thief spat on the floor in disgust at the troll's sword. "The blade isn't smooth."

A creature of the mist appeared. Its smokey gray body wrapped around the troll, and in an instant, they disappeared.

Reece swallowed but held in the breath he wanted to release as he watched the tall, gray-haired man yell at or praise the other swordsmith's work. He was glad he was at the end of the line. Only two others remained. He tightened his fingers around the handle of the katana he'd created. It wasn't quite finished, but he thought it was better than some of the other weapons presented. He glanced down at his foot. The tingle of awareness there of the dagger he'd concealed under his skin made him uncomfortable. He'd relied on the self-healing skin to hide the one weapon that could possibly kill the Overlord. He wouldn't reveal the dagger unless it was needed as a passage to get close to the Overlord. No one there had presented anything he felt would disqualify his work.

The older man stepped in front of Reece. He had to tilt his chin a bit to look at the Soul Thief eye to eye. "We don't see many humans here. I'll give you a break for that alone. You must be special for the mist to pick you to come here."

"My work speaks for itself."

"You from town? You in high school?"

"Newport, yeah. It's summer vacation, though."

The soul warrior glanced down at the katana. "I love those swords. For some reason, the magicals here don't make them. They aren't into swords since Merlin stole the ancient one they had in some sacred stone here. That wizard gives humans a bad name."

"Hmm." Reece thought it better not to reveal more through conversation, so he lowered his head, hoping the guy would approve of him and move on.

"You can stay. Finish the sword. It needs smoothing."

Reece waited until he heard the footsteps move away. Then he looked up at the group of guards.

"Those who were chosen to stay can perfect their weapons. Sleep here tonight. You aren't allowed to leave this room. Anyone who does will be killed by the guards on watch outside that door." The Soul warrior glanced at the weapon — "Not bad, not bad at all" — and pivoted away from him. "Feed them."

Reece sighed, then went over to his workstation to clean up. Before he could make it to his table, someone tapped him on the shoulder. He stopped, wondering if he should bother turning around. He knew the magical who'd stopped him. Reece found the scent of it earthy like grass with the gamey aftertaste of wormed-filled dirt.

"What?" Reece didn't want to talk; he needed to work on the sword and get into the wing where the Overlord resided. The entrance to the garden may be there, he hoped.

"I'm Quiver, and I wanted to tell you your work is unique."

Reece waved at Quiver to follow him. He didn't have time to waste on being idle. Also, he was getting hungry, and not for human food. Quiver could be his unsuspecting snack. Reece tossed the katana on the metal table, then turned to his meal. His incisors tickled his gums, and he stared at Quiver, who was a bit shorter than him. Gold hair and blue eyes on a fresh-faced teenager about Reece's age.

"What kind of magical are you?" Reece figured he should ask first to ensure whatever the guy was, wasn't poisonous.

"Leopard shifter, and you?"

"Human. Boring – nothing to see here, kind of magical." Reece laughed.

Quiver frowned. "Maybe, but —" his nose twitched — "I smell something beneath the surface. It's faint like there is a poison within you. Were you bitten by a werewolf? Vampire? You know they can mark you so they can come back later and finish the job."

Reece kept his expression stone cold. "I would know if that happened."

"Not necessarily. Vamps can take from you when you are sleeping, having sex with them, or just minding your business. Depending on the breed, a werewolf wouldn't let you survive. But the Dark Forest wolves like to scratch their victims then hunt them down to consume – even the bones – when the victim least expects it."

"And you are telling me this why?"

"Because I'm impressed and curious."

71

"Don't you have your uh – club to work on?" Reece had lost his appetite. Stealing magical essence from this guy would be a mistake. Quiver was too perceptive, and Reece couldn't afford to risk what he came here to do for a diversion into gluttony. His tingling tastebuds would have to wait.

Quiver shrugged. "It can wait."

"You! Human, your dinner is on the table in the corner." The young guard with almond-shaped eyes and a frown came over to them. His straight black hair, which was long on the top, fell over one of his eyes below the cropped sides of his haircut.

"Thanks." Reece glanced at Quiver. "I'm Reece."

Quiver smiled. "I knew you had a name. I'll get my meal and bring it over. They'll be locking us in soon anyway."

Reece grunted, not wanting to seem too pleased with the company. He went to the corner where there were several large pillows on the floor along with a bowl of stew with a thick piece of bread on top. Next to it was a glass of water with ice. Not bad. The stew smelled decent. Not that human food was something Reece found appealing much anymore. It did give him sustenance at least; the blood crystal necklace helped him stomach the unusually bland taste. He felt the heaviness of it deep within his skin. It had concealed itself for some reason. Reece had yet to figure out exactly how the necklace worked, but he knew Jeb told him he'd have to take it off one day.

Cracking his neck to the side, Reece plopped down on the large, firm pillow and crossed his legs.

"Good, there are three pillows here." Quiver sat next to him with a plastic container filled with raw ground meat, onions, peppers, and some garnish-like parsley on top.

Reece turned away as the blood in the meat tickled his nose. It wasn't appealing since the beef was dead. Forcing a smile of satisfaction, he picked up the stew.

"Are you always this friendly?" Reece tore off a piece of bread, dipped it deeper into the stew, then stuffed it in his mouth.

"Yeah, to my detriment most times." Quiver shrugged. "I am a bit more so now since my family died of the virus."

Reece frowned. "What kind of virus?"

Quiver nodded. "Oh, right, they protect you humans from what happens in The Void by making you think you live in Newport, RI." He laughed. "Stupidest thing in the world to do, but I just live here and don't make the rules." Quiver took a spoon full of his raw meat concoction and chewed. "It was a raging sickness among the shapeshifting magicals that mostly affected those of the leopard communities. Rumor was it was started here in a hidden lab where the Overlord has scientists doing unnatural experiments on magickind."

"Weren't you created by experimentation? I mean, magic was created by experimentation."

"You can say that the fallen ones used magic to create some of us, but natural magic was always around us. When magic created magic, we became creations born of love and shared energy. The forefathers who created us were no longer in control of what we became. Then certain species

73

of magicals could not produce children together, no matter how they tried."

"So, even here, there are those who would break the rules of your nature to create something of their own against those laws." Reece shook his head. "Not surprised."

"Well, someone who worked in the lab was attacked by a girl created there, and it ravaged my home, leaving only a few of us without the sickness. My brother attacked and ate my mother and sister. I escaped when he seemed to go into some type of trance when he was full of their flesh. I didn't get far from our village before the mist came for me to bring me here."

"How long have you been here?"

"This time, only for today. The last time, I impressed the Overlord with my sledgehammer, and I stayed a few weeks to complete several of them for his army."

"Is the virus gone?"

Quiver frowned. "We don't know. The horde was being rounded up and killed by the Soul Warriors." Quiver whispered, "It's the only reason I can tolerate them – knowing they at least had the power to kill the sick."

"Yeah, well, at least, there is that. But, aren't the Soul Warriors cursed?"

"Definitely. Poisoned with dark magic pulled from the place where our ancestors are imprisoned. Only humans can have a soul that can transport them there and return here alive. It's why the Overlord uses them. It's his way of stealing magic from the fallen ancestors. When he is done with the Soul Warriors, he kills them. Their magic has nowhere to go but into him."

Reece stopped eating. His brother Dexter had the Soul Thief's ring on his finger when Reece found him. Thank God he'd gotten his father in time to have it removed. He wouldn't want his brother to be like them. "Do they know they'll die in the end?"

"Of course not," Quiver laughed, "then they wouldn't sign up for the job."

"No, they wouldn't." Reece put down his half-empty bowl and shoved it away. Megan had lured him to do her bidding the same way. He hated feeling cornered, and now he was sandwiched between her will, his, and whatever Jeb wanted him to do. He'd become their puppet. No more. He would not give in until he got what he wanted.

Chapter 14

Everyone was asleep—or so it seemed—except Reece. He'd been slowly dragging in the essence of their magic to gain strength. Not that he needed it. Reece felt the throb of the magic he'd collected pump through his veins as if building up for some big moment. Hunger hadn't been tempting him. It was mainly all the tastes and flavors of magic that did. It wasn't like consuming food; every magical tasted different yet had similar qualities. He didn't hunger for the taste of any magical. There was magic that he didn't like the taste of or even want – that was whatever it was that hung around the Soul Warriors. The magic within them was putrid, rotten, and darker than any of the other magicals he'd sampled. The newness of his transformed body still amazed and scared him from thinking of the possibilities of what would happen after he saved his family. What then? No one to love – or that would love him. If the magicals knew he was born from the creature who started the disease they were still fighting, he'd be destroyed.

Reece wondered if the small percent of human blood he had left would allow him into heaven. He hadn't considered the condition of his soul since they'd been persuaded to move to The Void. Going to places of worship wasn't on his mind much when they moved, even though his parents were regular participants in a non-denominational worship center near their home in Brooklyn, NY. They never fully got involved but attended the weekly services on Thursday nights since his parents owned a mixed martial arts center and were busy on the weekends.

The snoring sounds of the others became rhythmic. Reece assumed they were all deeply asleep. He missed home so bad it felt as though a knife pierced his heart each time, he reminisced on anything to do with the place.

The guards' chatter could be heard from under the door. Reece had concealed a hook pick to unlock the door. He wondered why the magicals didn't use more magic. Maybe their laws prevented them, and the Soul Thieves arrested them for doing so. Reece closed his eyes and pushed his thoughts into the minds of the other three remaining in the room.

Sleep deeper.

Quiver murmured, but his snores got heavier.

Quietly, Reece moved. The soft-bottomed shoes Ora gave him were whisper-quiet. Time slowed, it seemed, but his steps were lightning fast, putting him at the door. He slowly opened it, noticing the two Soul Warriors. One was laying his shoulder against the door like he was catching a nap, and the other was playing with a whip at his side. Reece tried to force his thoughts into their minds and was slammed against a darkness that made him gag. An evil presence within their thoughts made Reece sense a demon's hold on them. Something he'd never considered could be a reality until he landed himself in the purgatory for magical creatures, which he now called home.

Reece thinned his lips. He couldn't get them to sleep. There was only one other option, knock them out or call DewOfWinter to take them away.

He thought of her and found his mind traveling above the mist over the bridge. Reece forced his command into her essence and felt her movement still then struggle before conceding. Reece stepped out of the room and reached his arm around the guard in front of him. Then he put his other hand over his mouth, hoping he wouldn't wake up the other guard.

The guard struggled and slammed back into the wall. Reece flinched at the power within him. If Reece were human, bones would have broken. He yanked the whip off the guard's waist. The guard slammed back harder this time.

Reece took the hit. He kicked the guard's back, forcing him forward. Stumbling, the guard growled. "Mando! Wake up!"

"Wha?" said the sleeping guard.

Where was DewOfWinter? "I need to know how to get to the garden."

"You are going to die!" The first guard charged Reece.

Reece flicked the whip; it wrapped around the guard's neck. The other guard grabbed Reece by the waist.

"He's the human! Can't kill him, remember!" The guard's hands were positioned tight around Reece's throat. "I don't care. If he moves one inch, I'll break his neck."

"Why?" Reece asked.

Reece yanked the whip and slammed the guard to the

ground.

"He is too strong to be human."

Mist filled the hall. Then DewOfWinter grabbed the guard behind Reece. They disappeared.

The other guard stood, smiled, and said, "No one to save you now."

"Or you!" Reece let the magic he'd consumed free in his veins. He grew, his teeth elongated, his fingernails curved. Reece fell forward into a flip and then kicked the guard in the stomach. The guard slammed into the wall. A look of shock and then horror passed across his eyes.

"What are you?"

"Your nightmare." Reece yanked the struggling guard up by the collar. The guard lifted his hand, and from his palm, a glob of blue light formed a dagger of shimmering blue.

Reece grabbed it. It burned then cooled his hand before it disappeared.

"How— How are you able to dissolve the darkness?"

"I don't know."

DewOfWinter appeared again. "You want me to take him?"

"Yes, and can you make them forget?"

She smiled. "I can do something better."

Reece released him. Her thick grey form slipped around the guard. His screams were smothered as DewOfWinter covered his body, and they disappeared.

Chapter 15

Reece exhaled. Discovering his abilities on the fly could be a deadly experience. The Soul Warriors couldn't be mentally persuaded, and they had a dark presence that presented a barrier to him. He smacked his tongue against his teeth. The aftertaste of the rotten energy that surrounded them trapped them and made his craving for blood and magic coil to a stop.

Not wanting to waste more time, Reece ran down the hallway, ignoring the lack of décor along the way. He tried each door of the few rooms in the corridor. They were all furnished, but the items were wrapped tightly in cloth as though the furniture was to be moved. The passage came to a dead end with a hallway between him and an enormous door shaped like the one used for bank vaults. It was round with chiseled magic enchantments written on it. Reece glanced down the hall on the left. It was dark but seemed to go on for over a mile. He looked to the right; that hall ended after several yards at a large window.

"What do you think you are doing!"

The hairs on Reece's neck rose. Ora. She'd found him. He took a few calming breaths, blocked his thoughts, and pivoted around.

"I am trying to find an exit out of here. I was dumped in the workroom and barely finished the final three. They would send me somewhere with the mist if I didn't impress them."

Ora had her arms crossed. Her hair was piled in a high puffy bun of tight curls, some of which escaped to frame her face. She had her steampunk glasses back on, covering up her glowing mismatched eyes.

"The only way in there—" she nodded toward the door that looked like it belonged in a bank safe— "is by invitation."

"Okay. I'll go back."

Her shoulders dropped. "You left without me. How did you make it all the way here safely?"

"Luck. I convinced a mist creature I was supposed to be making weapons for the Overlord, but my transportation got distracted."

Ora raised an eyebrow. "You think quick on your feet. Well, you still put yourself in danger."

"I like danger." He smirked at her, hoping to lighten the mood. His anger over her killing his former girlfriend dulled. It was still there as a reminder to be cautious, but now he had a purpose for Ora. He wanted her to destroy him, also. He was a danger to her kind, and the thought of returning to the Earth realm enveloped him in a profound sadness that nearly brought him to his knees. There was nothing and no one here for him, and returning with his family once he freed them was impossible.

She smiled. "Yes, I guess you do."

"I will play nice when we go back." He shrugged and walked around her, expecting her to follow.

Ora pushed past him, hitting her shoulder against his arm. "You follow me so it appears you are being chaperoned."

"Okay." Reece wondered if he should warn her that the guards were missing. He thinned his lips and figured it would be best she found out alone. Fewer questions for him.

Reece counted the times he heard Ora's heels hit the floor. She was angry at him. Why? He didn't know. He shouldn't be important to her goal. Unless Ora didn't trust him. Maybe she sensed caution with him. Ora was surprised he was alive. Reece wondered what would have happened to his family on the day of the crash if Hook had killed him like Ora demanded. Get rid of the evidence of their inability to keep a creature like Zamina from giving in to her nature and trying to feed off the innocent. Reece couldn't believe he'd thought a vampire could be in love. Especially one who started an epidemic like a zombie surge in the shifter community.

Ora's steps slowed. He wanted to wait to react to her response that guards were not at the door. Reece flexed his hand into a fist to calm himself.

"Where are they?"

He exhaled. "Who?"

"The Soul Warriors who should be here on watch."

"I don't know where they are." This was the truth since DewOfWinter seemed free of his control when he wasn't focused on her. He was usually unable to reach her when she was traveling from one destination to another in mist form.

"Something is going on with the Mist Ones. First, you get dropped somewhere without me knowing; then warriors go off their post."

"What do we do now?" Reece raised an eyebrow, trying to get her past the idea that the Soul Warriors and the mist creatures were acting out of character.

"You go inside. I'll stand guard here so when the other Soul Warriors come to check on you, they won't ask about the others. If they do, I will make up something to tell them."

"Don't they have the power to know if a magical is lying?"

Ora smiled. "They have no power over me. My magic is rare and deeply intertwined with my humanity. Since I've become a Vigilant, the dark energy within the Soul Warriors seems to shy away from me. It's like they avoid me but don't know why."

"I'm also a Vigilant, but I didn't notice that quality."

"It presents itself differently in everyone — especially those humans with magic residue within them. Since you are all human, you have no magical energy that makes the Soul Warriors desire to contain you."

Reece held back his response and then decided to put some distance between them. Her scent seduced him like no other, and he couldn't risk a moment of weakness at the distraction.

"Right, I better go in while everyone else is still resting."

She gave him a curious stare. Reece ignored the need to respond to it and opened the door quietly. He closed his eyes to touch the minds of those within and realized one of them was awake. Unfortunately for him, it was the one person who would ask questions.

Chapter 16

Quiver's eyes watched Reece intently. Ora followed him into the room. She stood next to him with her hands on her hips and her back straight. She insisted on wearing glasses even more imposing than her shimmering eyes. The others were standing up, waking from the drug-like sleep trance that Reece had imposed on them.

"The Soul Warriors will be here soon," she said. "Hurry up and get to work. I will make sure to get food brought in for you."

Reece frowned, wanting to ask her how she would do that, but he supposed she had contacts with the guards since she was posing as one. He would use that fact to his advantage if they continued to work together.

She left the room. Reece didn't turn at the stomping of her feet. He knew from instinct that she was angry with him and confused. He wouldn't tell her what happened, and she didn't push by asking. They'd had a truce, an understanding, at least for now. Reece walked over to his work area, ignoring Quiver. Without having to invade the shifter's mind, Reece knew the curious magical would seek him out for answers.

Reece picked up his chisel and started on the metal he'd

left on his table. He heard Quiver approach but acted like he had limited hearing and just ignored him, hoping Quiver would go.

He didn't. Reece felt the presence of the shifter behind him as Quiver was contemplating something.

"I know you left the room."

Reece dropped his chisel and picked up the discarded rag next to his hammer. "You do?"

"I heard you fighting the guards."

"Really?" Reece chuckled. "How did I do?"

"Someone helped you. I heard a voice, female – but not hers." He head-motioned toward Ora.

"Why didn't you come and help me then?"

Quiver came closer, next to Reece, and he tugged on his shoulder.

"I couldn't move. I can't explain it, but I was paralyzed."

Reece shrugged. "You think they put something in the food?" He tapped his chin. "I didn't feel anything."

"I heard your voice in my head." Quiver's eyebrow dipped as he narrowed his blue gaze at Reece.

"I am not interested in you in that way."

Quiver's jaw dropped. "Are you serious? Do you think I am attracted to you? A human?"

"You said it. I didn't." Reece smiled, noticing that Quiver didn't mention male. Interesting. Maybe, shifters didn't care whether they were male or female. Quiver thought Ora was attractive. The scent of his pheromones heightened when she came into the room.

"You know her? The female guard?" Quiver's throat moved as he swallowed.

"As a prisoner." Reece studied him. Something within him rose and yelled, *she's mine*. Reece shook his head. That thought couldn't take root in his mind or heart. Ora was the last person he should consider in that way. Especially since he wanted her to destroy him when this was done.

"I'd be her prisoner any day and make it worth her while." Quiver smiled. "I could make her want me."

"Aren't shifters supposed to bond with other shifters?" Reece smiled.

"I never said I would bond with her. Our numbers are lessened from the recent scourge placed on us by the virus. Besides, shifters prefer to bond with other shifters since it is easier to conceive. When we bond with other magicals, we will likely be childless unless we get help or, in a rare instance, it happens."

Reece chuckled. "I don't care about having children. I only want to be out of here."

"There's only one way to do that. Create something the Overlord wouldn't like but would put you at the mercy of the mist. The other is to give him something he will like enough to invite you to his wing."

Crossing his arms in front of Quiver, Reece asked, "Will they take more than one of us?"

"They'd like more than one since more weaponry will be created that way."

"Then yours better be good. Mine will get me there."

"Yeah, right, human." Quiver waved at him and pivoted away.

Reece exhaled and closed his eyes. Before he could turn around, Soul thieves, the males of the Soul Warriors, brought in trays of food. One of them tossed his on the table next to him.

"I'm surprised you survived. I heard your work was good."

"That's why I am here...I guess." Reece shrugged. He eyed the food. The thought of filling his mouth with the bland, pasty dead bread, stew, and apple made him wipe a hand down his face. It was substance and would stop him from salivating after Ora and the magic creatures around him. Her...she had a tinge of human blood within that made him even more hungry to taste. A flash of him pulling her close and kissing her sprang up in his mind. Reece shook his head to get rid of the thought even as his mouth watered at the temptation and forbidden desire.

He grabbed the bread and stuffed it in his mouth. No taste, no satisfaction, just something to fill his belly. The energy from the food kept his human side sated, but his beast raged. The angelic essence within him stayed dormant. It was so deep within him that he could forget it was even there. That side of him, he had no control. It expressed itself when it wanted, and most times, not at all. Reece wondered at that fact; maybe it was him. Reece felt that for the light within him to shine, he had to do something to be worthy of it. Reece had a feeling that would happen more often than he wished. The angelic essence presented itself as a protective system and was reactive to the nature of Reece's heart, his true nature. He didn't think it would allow Ora to destroy him even if he wished it to happen. Time would tell, though. The discoveries of the unique anomalies within him only revealed themselves when he was under the stress of life or death.

Without realizing it, he had finished all the food. He grabbed the cloth napkin from the tray and wiped his hands. Time was wasting, and he needed to get into the Overlord's wing. That was where Zamina's rooms were. It would bring him closer to finding the garden and alerting the Vigilant to attack. Reece may have to show his hand and reveal the dagger he'd made before his family's car had been attacked to get the Overlord's attention.

The blade he'd pierced the mermaid with would be impressive. Even the Merpeople were afraid of it when he wielded the weapon. He would wait until they had to show their latest creation before he revealed the blade.

Cracking his head to the side, Reece picked up the hammer and a discarded piece of metal. Time to pretend he was creating something incredible. The blade he made seemed to sense its days of hiding were over. The sharpness of the point was deep within the skin of Reece's shin. He'd hidden it there, thinking to take it out to attack. Now, it was his ticket, one step closer to bringing the war to the gates of the Overlord's hiding place. Reece smiled.

Chapter 17

It was time to show his hand. The Soul Warriors gathered, primarily males but some females. The guys looked like high school jocks in tailored outfits, similar to an off-duty police officer's. Comfortable, ready for a good fight, but all in the same black tapered shirts and jeans. Every one of the males had on a gold ring with a glowing blue orb in the center. It reminded Reece of a class ring for a graduate. The females were all tall and carrying themselves in a manner that wasn't manly but made it clear they could handle a good fight. They were beautiful with darkness shadowing them that was strongest around the necklace they wore with the same radiant orb that the males wore.

They weren't taking their guarding of them very seriously as they talked amongst themselves while throwing commands to finish up what we were working on soon.

Reece overheard them. They were concerned that the mist magicals were becoming unhinged and were no longer controllable. Especially since the other two guards were missing. Reece learned that those guards weren't the only ones to disappear. He'd wondered if he had corrupted DewOfWinter or if something else was going on. The Ashta leader might have started a revolt if his anger at the Overlord had been shared with his kind. Maybe he asked for their help in freeing his mate? Reece nodded to himself; that would help him in his cause. Maybe make the Overlord bring him closer into the fold so he could find where Zamina's wing was and the entrance to the garden maze.

While the others were busy and ignoring him, Reece bent down. He lifted the tapered bottom of his pants. Closing his eyes, Reece released the power he'd tapped down within him, and his fingernail elongated to a sharp-clawed curve. He swallowed the raging flow of energy bubbling up from his stomach and swiftly cut his skin. With its hooked tip and multi-colored metal, the blade dropped to the floor. Reece swiftly picked it up and put it in his belt at his waist. He felt the skin he'd severed stitch itself back together with a severe itch that caused him to press his foot into the floor to stop scratching it again.

"All of you! Get here and show what you have built," demanded the tall Soul Thief, who appeared to be the oldest. He had dark skin and stood a head taller than the others. His seven-foot frame was thick with muscles.

Reece walked over, sliding in the line behind Quiver. The Cyclops led the way, confident in the spiked, two-balls battle weapon he'd made. The cyclops' meaty hands grasped the handle wood that had two swinging spiked balls. He swung them, and they bounced off his back, leaving red marks that didn't bother him. It was impressive in size and made for a giant, but Quiver's battle-axe was better designed and more deadly. He'd had the double axe, with a knife that sprang out of the bottom, swinging at his side.

Reece had second thoughts about the dagger. The metal was uniquely powerful but was still fashioned to be deadly.

The curved, multi-colored blade vibrated from the energy and emotion of its handler. One side was smooth to perfection and could slice through flesh like butter.

"This is your weapon? Impressive." The tall Soul Trainer pointed at the cyclops' work. He picked it up, held it above his head, and then flicked it, causing the spiked metal balls to whiz through the air. He spun it so fast you could hear the whistle from the force of it.

"Is it good?" the magical asked, straightening his bare back.

"Decent, but not unique." The Soul Trainer lifted a hand and steepled his fingers. A thick smoke funnel materialized in front of the Cyclops.

He reared back as if attempting to run. The shape of a female formed from the thick smoke, and she laughed. It wrapped around him like a snake in an instant then enveloped the Cyclops in the middle. The mist dissipated with the massive creature with it.

Reece watched Quiver's handshake as he raised his weapon for inspection. Quiver was so distracted he neglected to show the blade he installed in the bottom of the battle axe. Reece whispered but projected the thought into Quiver's mind. *The hidden weapon, Quiver, show them.* Quiver jumped and whipped his eyes toward Reece.

Reece lowered his gaze to his feet.

"I can also do this with it." Quiver's voice was broken in his delivery until he cleared his throat.

"That's good. Real good. Take him to the Overlord, Nino."

An olive-skinned guy with a jet-black tapered cut and long bangs stepped forward and grabbed Quiver by the arm. "C'mon. Take your weapon."

Quiver bent to pick up his weapon and frowned at Reece.

Reece raised an eyebrow at him then turned to the tall Soul Trainer in front of him. "Here's mine." He reached to his side and slid out his dagger. The handle was intricately designed, and its curved, thick-backed blade glowed in a rainbow of color. Reece sliced it through the air, and the color changed with each movement.

"What the hell? How'd you get that? The metal for your weapon?"

Reece heard gasps around the room.

"Give that to me!"

Straightening his back, Reece held the weapon tightly. "No." He stepped forward. The power drumming beneath his skin was waiting for a reason to escape.

"I've got him." Ora's strong voice vibrated through the silence. "The Overlord would want to see the person who could touch that metal and shape it. The magic is strong and temperamental of its maker."

"I'd like to know how he got it. The rarest metal on this plane, and a human is shaping it?"

"It found me." Reece laced his voice with steel.

The Soul Trainer narrowed his eyes. "So, it has. Someone leads the cambion and the human to the Overlord's wing."

Reece stepped forward, but the Soul Thief caught him by the arm. "My name is Santtu. Don't forget it. We will meet again." The man's hand glowed, almost burning Reece's skin.

"You better hope not." Reece snatched his arm from the man's grip and narrowed his gaze at the other man's eyes widening. He tucked the dagger into his shirt, flinching as he pierced his skin and sank it into the cocoon of the wound he'd created. The skin bubbled and stretched as it covered the weapon. Only a few drops of blood stained his shirt. Santtu better forget him and stay out of his way. He was too close to getting the answers he sought and paying his penance for becoming a monster.

Chapter 18

They took Reece to the door he had seen. The one that appeared to be the entrance to a vault. The door had a dragon engraved into its center. Around it, realms on flat pieces of land were etched with different breeds of magicals on them. It was the entrance to the Overlord's wing where the dragon figure sprang from with its sunken eyes. The Soul Warriors and Ora stood in front of the door.

"Stand back," directed the guy in the front.

Reece was ready to get on with it but waited while he and the other guy held up their fists. They pressed their rings into the hallowed eyes of the dragon design etched into the door. The illuminated blue light from their rings seeped into the door, and the power from their dark magic filled the grooves of the etched art on the door. Their magic illuminated a map of all the realms the Overlord controlled. Faeries and the Fae were outlined in blue. Titans and Demigods seemed to float up from the art. Werewolf and vampire realms lit up, then the blue light shaped into a fire and rushed into the dragon's mouth. The door rumbled and slid into the wall.

Reece inhaled the smell. It was flat, tasteless, and heavy. The door opened, and they were outside. It couldn't be called a courtyard because it was a reasonable distance from the wing where they'd come. There were no flowers, nothing of beauty. It was a wasteland of thorn-shaped rocks with a backdrop of a glowing gray sky topped by a bright white moon to emphasize the hue of magic that seemed to hang in the air. Several yards ahead was a dark structure shaped like a castle. The moisture in the air hinted there was a water source nearby, although nothing could be seen beyond the cloud and mist surrounding the front of the structure. The ground had spears of rock on either side of the path and in front of the castle-shaped building. The clouds met the sharp rocky ground in patches and thicker covering to shield the space beyond the Overlord's home. Gargoyles sat on the curved ledges of the castle with giant Berserker statues on each side of the stairs leading to the door. Lightning jumped off the tips of the sharp rocks that covered the land. Reece smelled power, energy, and magic. Even the atmosphere held a green electromagnetic glow. It vibrated around them.

"Follow us," the taller Soul Warrior demanded.

"The energy here? It comes from the lightning?" Reece uttered.

"No, it comes from the Overlord. His magic and energy fuel this place and the entire collection of all the Realms. He controls it and creates with it. Takes it."

"Where does his magic come from?" The Soul Thief next to him frowned in annoyance.

"He was born through natural magic, a shifter who has created his own form. That has never been done before. Since that moment, his parents knew he was special."

"His parents, are they still here?"

"They were murdered. The dragons didn't like the fact that a born child had dominion and power over them. The former Overlord protected him. Then the current Overlord's wife betrayed his desire to seek the magic created by the Fallen. When she ripped the magic from him, the dragons took that moment to attack his castle and kill his parents and the army left to defend the realm. When the Overlord returned, he destroyed nearly half of the dragon's magicals and became the king."

"What happened to his wife?"

"He killed her and will likely never marry again," the Soul Trainer chuckled. "Women will be a man's weakest link if he chooses the wrong one."

Reece frowned; he understood that deception – too well. He followed the path with the others. There was obviously no way to escape. The trail was cleared; the thorn fields surrounding the castle and the entrance to the other wing would kill anything that tried to step on them. It was an obvious deterrent.

"Will I survive the meeting?" Reece figured he'd get as much information about the Overlord as possible, especially since this Soul Thief was willing to talk.

"Up to you. If you create his weapons and appear respectful of his position, he'll keep you alive until you are no longer useful to him."

"Is that so for you Soul Warriors also?"

The Soul Thief hesitated then said, "We all have an expiration date. When the Overlord wants more dark magic from the realm of hell his ancestors are trapped within, we, the Soul Warriors, are the only conduit between hell and The Void. His ancestors put their dark magic in us. We carry it and use it to contain you magicals. The Overlord siphons it from us if he needs a boost in magic to conquer attacking realms."

"That's horrible. Why would you let him use you like that and then kill you when he's done?"

The Soul Warrior gave him a sanguine smile. "We didn't, and here we are, too late to turn back, right?"

Reece fell silent. "Why tell me this?"

The Soul Warrior lifted an eyebrow. "I don't want you to have the same fate. I'm doing for you what I wished someone had done for me. If he offers to make you a Soul Thief – refuse even if it means your death. As a human, your humanity allows you to be saved in the end. And death is better than this."

"Tye! Go back to the main wing. I'll take it from here."

The Soul Warrior gave Reece a nod and then turned back down the path they came from.

Reece glanced up at the Berserker statue and could have sworn its eyes followed him and the others. Ora acted like she didn't know him, which suited Reece just fine. The remaining Soul Warrior stood in front of the door that mirrored the dark scene around them. It reflected back at them but erased their presence in the picture. If Reece hadn't known they were looking at a door, he would have thought that, beyond the frame, they were walking into another patch of thorns.

It opened. Inside, a large receiving area was artfully

created with wood walls and high-backed chairs of various designs and thicknesses. Some were large enough to seat giants, and others were tiny for small Faeries or mice. The floors were wood and steel with carpets arranged to separate the vast room into different areas. There were several levels up that could be seen from the walkways that allowed inhabitants in those rooms to look down by peering over the wood and twisted designed rail. The art adorning the walls was either paintings or tapestries. They were unlike anything Reece had ever seen. Each design seemed to beckon with a setting that, if you watched it long enough, started to come alive as though you were watching it from a window. The statues that went from floor to ceiling in each corner of the room were so lifelike they seemed impossible to have been made. With veins from one female dressed in warrior garb with wings and horns on each side of her head – to a Gryphon whose eyes weren't of steal or the stone it was carved from but seemed alive as if cast in its own prison. Reece felt the power emanating from them and knew, in some form, they were alive. He consumed a tiny bit of their magical essence and felt sated after an inhale.

"He will meet you here." The Soul Warrior waved his arm at the open room. "I'll stay, and one of his attendants will show you where to go."

"I'm staying with him. I was told to make sure he stayed alive." Ora turned to the Soul Warrior.

The man folded his arms. "A cambion? The only reason you haven't been killed by one of us is that you kept his abomination of a sister alive." He leaned forward. "Where is she now? I don't see her protecting you as if you were her last meal."

"Watch what you say. There are ears here, you know." Ora removed her glasses, and her glowing pupils made the Soul Thief step back.

"Fine, you present him to the Overlord. I'm out of here."

Reece waited until the guard stomped off and the door slammed. He stepped closer to Ora. "Do you know where they will put me?"

Ora shrugged. "No, I've never been here before."

They heard steps from above. Reece hesitated in looking up; he didn't want to be intimidated by what he may see. He couldn't help but hear the intake of Ora's sharp breath.

Reece closed his eyes and focused on what he was there to do. Whoever made Ora gasp wouldn't get the satisfaction of catching him off guard.

Chapter 19

Reece left his head bowed. He didn't want to upset the leader of The Void in any way. His deception of weakness had to be perfection. Multiple footsteps and a sliding noise announced their arrival in front of Reece.

He blinked and swallowed at the trio. One was a man with deep olive skin; long, thick black hair; and gray eyes that made Reece raise his hand to his neck against the intense pressure of an invisible force trying to push into the depths of his mind. Reece mirrored the energy with his own, giving a vision of a memory from his history class: his lively teacher dressed in garb from the seventeen hundreds while reciting a poem.

The man smiled, but it didn't sit within his gaze. Reece glanced at the two magicals at his side. One was a female with bright white shimmering skin stretched over her snake's lower body and rattled at the gold tip of her tail. Her breasts were adorned in a gold vest that covered her chest but hung low at her waist, synched with a red jewel embedded into her belly button. Her hair, eyes, and forehead were covered in a gold helmet. It didn't appear that she could see through it, but she moved as though she could. Reece swallowed; she had an old smell to her magic. It was appealing but not alluring like Ora's.

He turned, and his eyes rose to the giant man next to the Overlord. He had a covering over the bottom half of his face, below his red eyes. His hair was long and blue but waved in the air by an electrical surge of blue lights. The armor on him was silver and dug into his human-shaped chest from both sides, covering his arms, legs, and shoulder but leaving his chest bare. Reece frowned at the uselessness of armor that didn't protect vital organs.

"Do you speak?"

Reece cleared his throat. "Depends on if I have something to say."

"His talent for creating weapons is why he was chosen to come." Ora stepped to them.

Grabbing the dagger from inside his shirt, he twisted his wrist to present it to the Overlord with a flick to show off its blade and expose the hidden spiral blade that extended from the bottom of the handle. "It's deadly on all sides."

"That metal, where did you get it?"

"Someone left it in the scrap metal in the workhouse."

Reece didn't look at the Overlord. He didn't want the magical master to know he'd lied. He pushed the weapon forward as a distraction, an offering for the Overlord to take.

It worked; the heaviness of the dagger was lightened. The Overlord's fingers never touched Reece's hand, but the pressure from the power of his nearness pushed Reece's hand downward.

"Good work. More of it will keep you alive, human." The Overlord turned away. "Sleep tonight with the cambion as your guard. I will see you in the morning."

The male in the misplaced suit of armor stayed behind. Reece scented his magic, noting it was old and war-ridden. It flowed more easily around him than most magicals who weren't concerned about their magical essence being stolen. "You may take him to sleep in the wing through there." The magical pointed. "Do not go further than the front rooms. Your former charge's quarters are locked until she returns or the body is found."

"Of course." Ora waved at Reece to follow. She walked through the open area of the receiving rooms to a large door on the far end. Ora turned back at the massive male with her hand on the door.

"Just turn the knob; it was open in preparation for the swordsmiths. Another is already there in his room. Once you enter, you can't come out unless summoned."

Reece frowned. He'd have to find a way.

"The Mist Ones? Why couldn't they bring us here?"

The red-eyed guard's eyelids dipped. "They've been troublesome of late. But if you don't perform, the Overlord may give you to them – for a meal."

Reece nodded and followed Ora through the door. This hall was in a darker wood tone; the walls appeared neglected of cleaning, and the wood appeared aged. There were no paintings or decorations except on the ceiling. Metal panels with imprints of various weapons adorned the ceiling, making it an interesting piece of art, from the arrangement of each panel to the imprinted design within each of them.

"Let's take this room. I don't sense anyone's presence

here." Ora led Reece several yards into the hall. "Quiver is in the first room."

Reece hadn't been paying attention to where they were going; he'd been studying the art, getting ideas on what he could make to impress the Overlord, maybe get him to trust his work. They walked into the room. There was one bed in the middle. The place smelled like it had been cleaned with pine and lemon. A couch sat in the corner and a fireplace stood on the opposite side of the bed. The bed had a padded backboard of soft white leather and suede. There were no pictures on the walls and no windows.

"You don't want your own room?" Reece leaned against the door to close it. He crossed his arms in front of him and waited for a response.

Ora's eyes darted around the room, and she sighed. "I don't trust that you won't run off again or do something stupid that will endanger the reason we are here."

Reece sensed a tension deeper than her words, a wanting desire she tried to hide. He wondered if his vampire blood made her act this way. He decided to press his assumption. "I think you desire my company, maybe my closeness more than lack of trust."

She pursed her lips. "Not likely. I didn't like you for Zamina, and I don't want you for myself. You couldn't be with me anyway. I'd hurt you."

Reece smiled at that last comment. If she only knew. He watched her swallow and turn away to walk to the nightstand next to the bed. "Liar. I know there is a thin line between hate and attraction. I feel there is some of both between you and me."

Ora sat in the chair. Her hand played with the steampunk-style glasses she hid behind. "I'm not..." She cleared her throat. "I am not interested in your games. I only want your forgiveness so we can move on to what we came here to do."

"Forgiveness. I am trying, but that comes with trust. Find another room." Reece slowly walked toward her. Ora stood her ground. She was beautiful, but he didn't think she knew it. Her soft brown skin and full lips, the shade of muted pink, quivered with each inch he closed between them.

Ora sprang up. "I will not. You escaped and would have ruined everything if I hadn't found you." She held her hands at her sides and fisted them while her back was straight. "I could hurt you, make you listen with a flick of my wrist. I don't want to hurt you."

Reece smirked. He stood close to her, so close he could smell the sweetness of her breath and the essence of power within it. Before he could stop, he pulled her close and kissed her, slowly pressing his lips to hers, expecting Ora to push him away. She didn't. Instead, Ora whimpered, and her body shook with constraint. She wanted to touch him. He heard it deep within her thoughts she didn't feel safe expressing. He closed his eyes and inhaled more of her magic, her essence, and, God help him, he wanted more.

Deepening the kiss, he pressed his body against hers and, without thinking, spoke into her mind, *Touch me.*

She stilled and pushed him. Reece fell back, stumbling from the force of it.

"What? How did you speak to me? Kissing me – could

109

kill you."

He swallowed and righted himself. "What are you talking about? I told you that forgiveness…"

"Not that! You told me to touch you!" Her hands were fisted at her sides. Her body vibrated as though she held all of her power and magic from bursting outward.

"You sure you didn't read my thoughts? Why would I tell you to touch me when it's clear you don't find me attractive?"

"Uh!" Ora pushed past him. "I will be guarding the door. Get some sleep."

Reece chuckled as the door slammed.

Chapter 20

He couldn't leave her out there too long. Heartlessness wasn't going to sit in his new body, not with his human side still present. Reece needed time to process what he'd done. Part of it was fueled by the challenge within her, knowing that, at some level, they were interested in each other in a physical way. He'd felt it from the moment they first met, but she'd always had a barrier up. He understood that it had been to protect herself from rejection and the danger she felt her kind would be to anyone, magical or human.

Reece glanced around the room. There may have been a way to get out, without going through the door they were warned wouldn't open. They moved furniture around, realizing that the room could accommodate normal-sized people and a giant-sized magical if needed. The doorknobs were high, mid-level, and low. He went to the closet and searched the ceiling. It was a nice-sized walk-in closet with clothes of different sizes and types. Drawers for shoes of all sizes, from tiny for Faeries to massive for giants. He grabbed the ladder in the corner and moved it next to the wall. There may be a hidden passage in the wall.

Reece contemplated giving her another few minutes to cool off, but he didn't want to be at odds any longer.

Forget about it. He'd let Ora in and maybe come up with a plan. He opened the door, and she stood there with her back straight, arms crossed, and tapping her feet.

"I'm sorry."

She jerked around and frowned. "For what?"

"Kissing you without permission."

Ora raised an eyebrow. "Let's forget about it."

Reece opened the door. "My kiss was forgettable?"

"I don't know. It's my first one, so I will never forget it."

"Wait? You had a boyfriend. A few boyfriends in school. They never kissed you?"

She removed her shoes and eyed the bed. "You want to sleep in the covers or out of the covers? I can sleep under them and you sleep on top so we don't confuse things."

"You can get under the covers. I'm not cold." He hadn't felt hot or cold in what seemed forever. The only thing that warmed him was when he stole magic and bit his sister. Reece had only sunk his teeth in one other person. His best friend, Hook, let him practice control of his urge before Jeb allowed him to go home. Hook was a werewolf and recovered quickly from his bite, but Reece didn't find his taste appealing.

"I am going to take a shower." Reece walked to the attached bathroom to fight his urge to kiss Ora again.

He made quick work of getting undressed and showering in hot water. The steam around him felt nice, and washing his hair made it easy to comb the kinks with his fingers. He'd closed his eyes and felt her presence just outside the door. Ora wasn't in bed. Reece smiled. He opened the glass door to the shower and stepped out. He heard a gasp. Served her right for peeking at him. He wrapped his waist in a towel and grabbed his clothes off the floor. Opening the door, he noticed Ora on the other side of the room, looking through a dresser drawer and pulling out clothes.

"The male clothes are in the dresser on the wall near the bathroom." She didn't turn to face him but pointed to the left corner.

"Is that what you were looking for?" Reece chuckled; he couldn't help it. He felt the tension of her guilt, desire, and curiosity in the air. Ora must think Reece was weak, a human who couldn't be her equal. He couldn't promise her love, but he could be a companion until she gave him the end he wanted after he finished his purpose in The Void. In truth, he felt loneliness and a chill he hadn't felt ever before. Having a twin gave him a connection to someone all his life. That connection was broken because of his deceit and the monster within him. Rei may never really trust him again. He remembered how she hadn't wanted to come to his room after that incident or talk to him like she used to. Even though Rei never mentioned it, he'd hurt their relationship, and she'd shut that connection between them because of it.

Reece pulled up the shorts he'd found and walked to the bed. Ora turned around. Her large curls fell from the buns she had on the sides of her head. The girl didn't realize she'd taken his breath away. She may have thought she was stronger than him, but he'd unsettled her even with being what she considered a helpless human.

"I'm going to take my shower. You can go on and sleep. I'll be back after soaking in the tub." She pressed her lips together and walked past him without a glance.

He smirked. A challenge; he liked that. Reece grabbed the blanket from the nightstand. He climbed onto the bed; it was high and had stairs on the side for normal-sized people. The bathroom door creaked open. Reece, pretending to be asleep, closed his eyes. Lying still while Ora moved about the room and put things away was oddly soothing. The bed barely moved as she joined him there. He felt the covers being lifted when she slid beneath them. Ora hesitated and moved closer.

Reece opened his eyes, and she scrambled back. He grabbed her hand and tugged her closer. "Friends." He smiled. "I won't kiss you unless you ask me to."

She narrowed her eyes. "Why would I beg you to kiss me?"

"I didn't say beg. Just say, 'kiss me.'" Reece glanced down at her lips and felt her move slightly forward. Then she backed away from him, but her hand remained in his.

Ora nodded. "Friends. Not Frenemy, after what I've done?"

"Just friends. I've realized I have no right to persecute you if I don't want to be. I've made some horrible mistakes. My family is dead or in danger because of my selfishness."

"What mistakes have you made that you won't share? You've seen me at my worst."

"Have you ever killed before you killed Zamina?" Reece released her hand.

She sighed. "Never. I practiced it a lot as a guardian for Zamina, with my father, to defend myself against other magicals. My father warned me that I could do it without realizing it if I didn't contain my abilities. None of us have the same abilities. Most magicals know I am a cambion and are spooked by it. We are considered bad luck, sick magic. A total rogue magical."

"No friends then?"

"None. Even Zamina wasn't really a friend. She needed my magic to feed her, calm her, and allow her to be around others. She didn't have friends either but mostly seemed to accept her fate – until she met you."

"You never wondered about your mother?"

"Yes, but I am told human mothers do not survive the bird of a cambion. My heart ached for her then my father. Watching them kill him in front of me, I'll never forget it."

"How'd you meet Jeb?"

"Hook took me to him. Hook was a recruiter to the Vigilant. He made it his mission to recruit any magical who had human blood. He wanted them to be saved like he was."

"Are you free?"

She smiled. "Yes, in my heart, my mind, and spirit. I still have the magic, the darkness, but it doesn't control me. Also, most of all, I am no longer alone. I have a kinship with the Vigilant, something I can never have with other magicals. Being alone now isn't so bad."

"Well, no, you aren't. You have friends like me." Reece thought about her words, and though he felt a grounding with becoming Vigilant, he still felt alone, empty, and disconnected.

"Yeah, right? Friend." Ora yawned. "I'm going to sleep."

"Do you need a kiss goodnight?" He winked. "Friends are always ….

She closed her eyes and surged forward with her lips. Reece wondered if he should tease her or make her say the words, but instead, he kissed her back.

Chapter 21

Breakfast had been left in front of their door. They ate it silently in the room. Reece felt hesitant to discuss or repeat the kiss they'd shared before Ora pushed him away and muttered that the second kiss was better.

He felt a bit used when she said that. She treated him like he was someone to test her skills on. Something in him seized in his chest. It felt like jealousy, but why should he be jealous? Ora couldn't be more than she was for him at this moment. Not with their pasts, what she'd done, and how he had been deceiving her about his condition.

They opened the door. Quiver was standing there with his hand raised, ready to knock. He cleared his throat. His jaw dropped as he turned toward Ora then jerked his head to stare at Reece.

Ora pushed Quiver and stormed to the door at the end of the hall.

Reece shrugged. "She thought I would try to escape, so she guarded my door until I asked her to come in."

"Sure." Quiver pulled on his brown vest. His loose pants tapered at the ankle within his boots. "Let's go to the door of the hall. They'll be opening it soon."

"The weapon you presented was creative."

"What did you make that got you here?"

"A dagger."

"Must have been some special dagger."

"It was the metal. I believe it's called magniton." He remembered the name from Jeb, who'd given him the metal to make a sword he was going to sell. Ora was the one who held that sword to slice off the head of the vampire who made him.

"Magniton? Were you able to touch it? Impossible. That metal chooses who can wield it. The Overlord is rumored to have limited amounts of it since it is born of dragon bones."

"Hurry! I hear someone at the door." Ora waved at them.

Reece and Quiver jogged to her side, stopping just as the door swung open. They looked up and saw no one.

Someone cleared his throat. Reece looked down to find a short, stocky, old man with purple hair that whipped up on the sides. He had a long beard that fell to his belly. He wore leather-trimmed pants, a matching shirt, and boots with small heels. On his head was a copper-colored hat with a band around this forehead for small tools. His pants had a tool belt that held various instruments swinging beneath his crossed arms.

"Are you ready?"

"Yes." Ora nodded.

Reece inhaled; the power within this Gnome was strong, old, and contained. He was unlike most of the other magicals Reece had met, who felt no intimidation by his human appearance, so he allowed their essence to fall loosely around him. This Gnome had a barrier around him. Reece couldn't steal any of his magic without the Gnome feeling it. So, he backed off and observed.

With extra-long, crooked fingers, the little man lifted his forefinger and bent it. "Follow me."

They quietly walked through the main receiving room. The room was lit well, but the windows revealed a gloomy sky and rain outdoors.

"The Overlord isn't in the best mood. Someone has been stirring up the dragons to attack the weapon's stores and the tunnels where we mine minta-crystals for camouflaging magicals. The scientist still needs to learn how to pull that off, but creating weapons is what you are here to do. Sadly, there aren't many skilled in what the Overlord needs."

They came to a dead end. There was a giant statue of a man with the torso and tail of a scorpion that was sunk into the wall. He had a long curly beard and angry eyes.

"The statue?" Quiver asked.

"The Overlord's father before he was eaten by one of the Dragon King's warriors."

"They lost the war, right?"

"Yes, but at what cost? Nearly destroying a source of magic that could never be replenished. Killing the dragons nearly destroyed all the realms. Now, they are bitter and waiting for the chance at revenge. The worst kind of enemy to have."

The Gnome waved his hand, and a white glow illuminated the statue's base. It slid to the side. Reece turned and watched the panel in the wall close. He walked first through the opening and waited for the others.

"Was that the only way?"

"No, I prefer taking shortcuts. We are going to the weapons wing; the Overlord will meet us there after his briefing with the twelve. It's always chaos when the leaders from the other realms visit their representatives staying here. Everyone wants something." The Gnome snorted.

The pathway was made of smoothly carved rock and lined with candles for light. They were led through the first door before the bend in the tunnel. The room was enormous and took up three floors of the castle. It had multiple ovens, shelves of tools, and metals on built-in shelves on the wall. Some ladders went to each level. The walls were a dark gray and appeared to be carved from rock. There were dark smudges on the surface near the brick stoves that were already fired up.

Reece wondered where the others who would be working there were. He went to one of the tables and grabbed a leather apron. "What does he want us to create?"

Quiver walked over to Reece and turned toward the Gnome.

"Swords, daggers, and armor. When taking the war to the Earth Realm, some of their magic may be muted when they cross over. It is rumored that his deceased wife's spirit protects the veil and absorbs some of the magic from the beings who cross over. To regenerate magic depends on each magicals' ability, and we can't conclude how long there will be a weakness."

"When we are finished here, can we be returned to our homes?" Quiver picked up the other apron.

The Gnome grunted. "That is not guaranteed. You will be expected to support the battle by continuing to create the weapons needed. The skill is dying, and using magic to create weaponry isn't the same. Some materials the Overlord wants you to shape don't bend to magic, only by the bare hand."

"Are there others who will be here to help us with production?" Reece wanted to know because he needed to feed on their magic. Gaining all the strength he could through their essence would make it easier for him to use his abilities and conceal himself.

"Yes, soon. My name is Wykwor. I wanted to bring you both here first so you know what is expected of you." He turned to Ora, gave her a nod, and whispered, "The Vigilant doesn't have much time. This is as far as I've been able to get any others. The war is upon us sooner than we anticipated. Work together and trust no other. We are the only ones who have made it this far." The Gnome winked. "There are tunnels through every floor made by the mole shifters who were used to mine crystals for their magic. Those areas aren't protected. Use them to get around. There is a hidden entrance or trap door to them in your rooms. Move at night, be back by day, and if you encounter a Soul Warrior or magical, you must destroy them, or they will alert the Overlord's protectors."

"Megan, does she have people here watching me?" Reece asked, wondering if Megan had given in to her threat.

"The girl? Daughter of a Rumpelstiltskin? We don't

need her kind involved in this. I wonder if she has infiltrated. I will find out and try to divert any work to her cause."

"You..." Wykwor pointed at Reece. "He will want you to work with more of the magniton metals that are mined. Be cautious of the crystals. They can hurt humans, distort your reality, and burn your skin. Handle it with care if he tells you to touch any. The crystals also choose who can handle them; some magicals have even been destroyed."

"Will there be guards?" Ora bent down to ask. "Since I was Zamina's protector, I can try to convince them to give me more freedom around the castle."

"Yes, there will be guards. Try to move about since they consider you part of their inner circle, but you two go at night. And try to get close to the Overlord; find a weakness. There is a reason he needs someone who can shape the magniton."

Reece crossed his arms as Wykwor and Ora turned to head toward the door. He exhaled and reached for the sledgehammer on the table.

"I would've never thought you were a Vigilant," Quiver whispered.

Reece shrugged. "I am many things." He smirked. Being a Vigilant was likely the least of Quiver's concerns.

Chapter 22

They'd been working on creating something that would impress the Overlord. Reece watched the others, who made many weapons, but he had to create something that would get the Overlord's attention. No one really spoke while they worked. Quiver and he exchanged tools here and there. Reece was still pondering who to trust and realized he had few options. He had to work with Quiver, Ora, and Wykwor. He had to find a way to ensure that, if he got noticed, the Overlord would reveal a weakness.

Reece prided himself on creating weapons that had hidden features. He was impressed with Quiver's design and realized they had a similar style. Reece made a katana sword that, when twisted, had small spikes in the meat of the blade. He wouldn't finish it that day, but the weapon's shape would be evident. He heard rising voices behind him.

"He's here," others muttered.

A quiet fell over the room. The presence of the Overlord could be felt, and Reece stopped arranging his tools to see the king of this realm walk in with his two guards. One was a Cyclops, the other a Berserker. Each was huge in size and thickness.

"I am Cyrillus, the Overlord to the Veil. You were brought here because of your talents for creating weapons. Some of you will be moved to our training site to work with my captain. Those of you who have chosen to work with her, be warned to stay on her good side. She's been known to petrify those who displease her into stone."

Someone yelped. Reece didn't need to look; he knew it was the minotaur who was part donkey. That one had been skittish when they dragged him into the work area that morning. The Soul Warriors who had been guarding them stepped out of the room and closed the door. Cyrillus slowly perused the room with his eyes, staring at each chosen person as if assessing them and their magic. Reece felt a quiver in the essence of each that Cyrillus observed. He hoped the stone did its job and concealed his change well.

"You, human"—Cyrillus' eyes narrowed—"with a hint of something else. There must be something different about you that the magniton allows your touch." His eyebrow rose.

"Aren't we all different in some way?" Reece relaxed his muscles. He didn't want to show his hesitation; the Overlord was very observant.

"You are funny. Sure, of yourself?"

"No, but I am passionate about my craft. That may be why the metal chose to let me work with it. It feeds off the one who shapes it."

Cyrillus' dark eyebrow lifted, and his extended finger tapped his chin. "Good deduction. You, come with me."

Reece walked behind the Overlord, and the cyclops guard followed behind him. When he crossed the doorway, he saw Ora talking to one of the Soul Warriors. They all stopped and gave Cyrillus a quick bow. Reece noted that the man's hair was long like his, and the thickness of it barely moved as he walked. Reece had braided his hair to keep it out of the way while he worked.

The hall was much different than the tunnels from which they'd entered the wing where they created weapons. It had wood floors with deep red, gold, and silver designed carpet in the middle. They entered an open room with doors that went from floor to ceiling. Those doors were ajar and slid into the doorframe. Just the handles were visible. The room had red wallpaper that resembled cloth. The floor was trimmed in wood. A decorated burgundy rug with gold diamond-shaped designs in the shapes of different species of magicals lay in the middle. A single chair sat upon a platform in the back of the room. The chair was oversized, high-backed, and had thick gold handles. The surrounding walls had gold trim; high ceilings were painted with the designs of the magical realms over which the Overlord reigned. One wall held windows with open curtains, letting the moonlight shine on the floor. Under the moonlight, magical creatures and shadowed figures moved within the diamonds in the carpet. Reece blinked his eyes, wondering if there were actual magicals trapped in the carpet or just a play with the light from the moon. Paintings of former kings and queens adorned the wall.

Reece studied the last painting of the Overlord, much younger looking, holding the hand of a brown-skinned woman who had thick, tightly curly hair which fell to her hips. Braids, with gold intertwined, adorned the sides of her hairline. She gazed at him with adoration in her eyes and his of mischief.

The Overlord sat in the chair on the raised platform. The Berserker was next to him, and the Cyclops stood at the door. Reece bowed slightly, although it went against everything within him to do so.

"Okay, what happens now?" Reece waited for the Overlord to come out with what he wanted instead of threatening him with it.

"I am wondering why you have a familiar look to you. Your name?"

Reece considered his question and decided to give his middle name, which included his mother's maiden name. "You can call me Cade Abara." He fought against the urge to swallow after saying it. Then he decided to lead the conversation to a topic that was safe. "What would you like me to create for you with the metal?"

"A breastplate that can hold crystals. It must be thin enough to be comfortable but thick enough to protect."

"I can do it."

Cyrillus smirked. "I believe you can, but I wonder what else you can do. Tell me, where did you learn this skill?"

"I don't remember. I only know I woke up here." Reece hated lying, but this was life or death, so he made amends with himself for it. Avoidance he could stomach, but the outright lie was the only resource he had to get him through this mild interrogation.

"Funny, I can't seem to read you or your thoughts. What could be keeping me out?"

"There is a fog to my memory. Maybe you are experiencing that also?"

"No, there is a barrier, and it is strong." Cyrillus tugged at his neatly cut beard. "But, in time, it will break."

Reece nodded. "I'm sure it will. When would you like me to start?"

"Soon. For now, finish the weapon you are making. You can work on more of the metal when we acquire more."

"Overlord? I know very little about this place or how or why I would be here. I thought I was having a dream when I saw all the magical beings here."

"Humans come here either by accident or coercion. They could be here by a magical." He raised his eyebrows. "Or they have a purpose that serves me in being here. Magicals gaining entrance to your realm is more challenging. In some ways, there are anomalies to the protections erected to keep us out or for overrunning the veil between both realities. I assure you; this isn't a dream."

"Where is your queen?" Reece glanced at the portrait of the Overlord and his wife.

"You haven't heard the rumors? Well, I guess magicals aren't that friendly to humans. The queen is deceased. I sought to gain power in this world, to avenge those who killed my parents. It was dangerous and, I'd admit, risky for all magicals and humankind. My wife loved her people. She was a human, a gift of truce between our people. The bargain was that we stay here, and they would leave us alone. That never worked out as meddling magicians like Merlin wanted the magic with the power that came with it.

But I digress; my queen sought to stop me and threw herself at me, absorbing one of this realm's most powerful sources of magic. It killed her, and she died in my arms—the only woman I've loved and my betrayer."

"I'm sorry. You have no heir?"

"No, I am not ready to let another woman into my space. I enjoy them, but only for a time." He smiled. "And you, what do you want from your visit with us? Are you interested in gaining skills in magic while you are here? Merlin has protégé he sends here for those skills."

"I don't want to be a mage. I want to survive this and find my way back home."

"Well then, we must work on getting your memory restored. Then, maybe, your mind will let me in."

Reece's gaze clashed with the Overlord's. *You won't get in, ever.*

Chapter 23

Exhaustion wracked his body, but he couldn't afford to sleep too long. He rested against the wall with his hands fisted at his sides, trying to clear his head and stave off the rumbling of his stomach. His meeting with the Overlord had taxed his strength and made his hunger rise again. It didn't help his cravings with Ora nearby. When he'd arrived, she was finishing up the dinner that was left in front of their door. He hadn't eaten much because he didn't want the food they provided; he wanted blood and magic. Needed it if he were to meet with the Overlord again.

"So, what did you think about him?" Ora climbed into the covers on the bed. Reece's nose flared; she looked so tempting sitting there, oblivious to the danger she was in.

Swallowing the bile that bubbled up from remembering his encounter, he walked over to the bed and sat on top of the covers. Reece moved closer to her so he could inhale the magic she released when she spoke. Hopefully, that would sate his need. Kissing her was another way he could siphon some of her magic, more than remnants from her natural release of it. Maybe he could convince her to kiss him again tonight.

"He's bitter. I had to tell him I had amnesia. I don't think mentioning my father's name would be a good idea. So, I gave him my middle names."

"You have more than one?" Ora smiled. "How?"

"My brother and I have my mother's maiden name as one of our middle names. I told him my name was Cade Abara. He didn't trust it. I could see it in his dead eyes."

"We won't make it out of here alive if he has any doubt about our loyalties." Ora's eyes darted to his lips.

Reece smiled. "Then we won't give him doubt. I have to go exploring. Zamina knew a way out of here. There are no Mist Ones here. I don't think they know the way."

"Likely not. It's the Soul Warriors who bring people here."

He moved closer to her. "We need to find the garden entrance. That will be the way in the Vigilant need."

"Okay, I will try to get some clues from the Soul Warriors or other magical guards."

"I thought they would want you to stay with the other guards. Why did they let you return with us?"

"I spook them. The cambion, the magical leper. They are only polite because they know I was Zamina's keeper. The Overlord dealt with me but is angry that I 'lost' his creation. If he realized I killed her, he would try to destroy me."

"He thinks Zamina is just missing?"

"Yes, he knows she got out without notice. They were never on good terms. Zamina hated being treated like she was under scrutiny. Especially after she was initially the cause of the deaths of so many shifters."

"Then why would he want her in the palace?"

"Probably because she was going to be one of his weapons."

"After we get through all this, what will you do?"

Her eyes watered. She licked her lips as her eyes closed. "I don't know."

"If I asked you to do me a favor, something important, would you?" Reece wanted to see how she would respond and if he could trust her to follow through.

"It depends." She opened her eyes and turned toward him.

"That's an honest answer."

"When this is over, you will be with your family. You will be free of Megan and the Overlord. I promise I will do everything to help you. It doesn't matter what happens to me. No one will grieve me." A tear fell from her eye.

Reece wiped it away with a finger. "Yes, someone will." He leaned in and kissed Ora while pulling her into his arms. With each touch of her lips, he drew in more of her magic, and when she relaxed her lips, letting him delve in, it was as if she was giving her magic to him. He felt drunk on it and sated. Holding her close to his body, he flipped her to lie on top, nourishing his need to feed. Reece kissed her deeper and deeper until she sighed, and he felt as though he never wanted to let her go. His heart beat faster, which was something it hadn't done since he'd been infected. At last, he felt sated but kept kissing her just because he wanted to feel her lips touch his one more time.

He held her close as she slept. Without realizing it, she'd

given him more strength and sustenance than he needed. Kissing her was like a drug. Ora's magic was stronger than she knew. Reece had to use mammoth strength in stopping his incisors from extending. The need to taste her blood was so strong. Reece felt revived, tingling as though he'd drunk six cups of coffee, and he hated the taste of the stuff. *Sleep, beautiful.*

Ora's hand loosened its grip on his hair and fell to the pillow. He smiled at kissing her to sleep. Now he could go exploring and not worry about her safety. The tip Wykwor gave on the secret passages made Reece think about all the places he'd searched in the room. The one place he hadn't looked was behind the clothes, the dressers, or the armoire that was in the closet. Reece slid off the bed as gently as he could.

The closet was packed with clothes. Reece moved them aside and knocked on the wall to seek a hollow sound that would indicate an entrance or hidden exit. Nothing. He went to the armoire and moved the drawers. Noticing the drawers pulled out, he moved them around. Reece closed them and the door then tried to move the armoire; it wouldn't budge. The wood was thick and heavy, but he knew he was strong enough to move three times his size. Then he realized the armoire was attached to the wall. Reece took everything out of it and set it on the floor. The drawers wouldn't come out unless broken. He knocked on the back of it, thinking there was a trick door. There was no hollow sound.

"Damn!" He kicked the door then slumped against the wall. Hitting his head on the wall, he noticed the echoing thud. In the corner, he spotted a tear in the wallpaper. Reece pressed the surface with his hand. Under the small tear in the wallpaper, he realized there was an area with a thin indentation. He pushed it. The armoire sank into the wall. It was an entrance to a tunnel half his size. Reece had to get on his knees to slide into it.

The tunnel was dark, cold, and moved at random angles. Reece's ability to see clearly in darkness made it easy for him to crawl quickly. He heard voices ahead, making him slow his movements to ensure he wouldn't be detected. The covering ahead was thin, allowing light to faintly illuminate the tunnel. It must have been a picture or something in front of the hidden entrance. Reece stopped and lay on the floor of the tunnel and listened.

"If the Overlord wants this war with the humans, who am I to stand in his way?"

"I am not requesting that of you, I am asking that we slow his pursuit to make sure we don't end up like our ancestors in the abyss. His madness for revenge and power could lead to the demise of all of us."

"Very well, I will take council with him and have my gifts to the cause delivered within the next few weeks. This storage room needs cleaning and organizing if we are to transport weapons from here to the training grounds."

"We have a delivery going out with the captain later today. We will also have more shipments from the Vampiric Realm later today."

Someone snorted. "Why are they here? Whenever their king comes, I swear people go missing. He can't be trusted."

"He's in alliance with the Overlord. Remember the

Overlord's adopted sister was created from his blood."

"And what good did that do us? She started a virus that is still said to be wiping out pockets of shifters."

"The Soul Warriors have it contained. I hear the sister disappeared."

"Good riddance. Many thought they should have destroyed her. I don't know why the Overlord allowed his head scientist to further tamper with her."

"I've been here for a long time. The scientist is working to create crossbred magicals. It's groundbreaking research since it is rare that magicals of different species can procreate. Maybe the Overlord is trying to find a way to create an heir. I hear he was cursed barren after his queen died."

"That's old news. If he dies in this war, there will be no magical strong enough to hold the power of the realms together. We'll all perish."

"Oh, there is one other who is strong enough. He hates her, and if he can find a way to destroy her power, he would."

"I'm sure."

"Well, if that's all I can do for you, I'll take these weapons and prepare them for shipment."

"Good, good."

Reece waited until there was silence and closed his eyes, pushing one of his nails with its razor-sharp tip into the fabric. Since he didn't hear voices any longer, he peeked through, to discover he was under the floor. He laid his hand on the coarse underside of the rug and pushed it aside. Grasping the sides of the opening, he pulled himself up and out of the tunnel. Boxes, trunks, and bags of various things that appeared to have no significance to what he was looking for took up the space. Maybe the place had a map of the grounds somewhere. It would if they had to make deliveries. Reece slowly crept through the randomly placed boxes and shelves. He heard the shuffling of someone on the other side of the room. He'd tried to avoid them.

Silently, he moved toward a desk in the middle of the chaotic storage room. There had to be something there he could use. Reece squatted to the ground and rose at the desk's edge. Waiting a moment longer, he heard the steps grow faint as the person managing the place walked farther away. He stood, looking on the desk for anything of use. A book, like a delivery logbook, was open; a feather-tipped pen lay on it. He flipped back a few pages and slowly tore out several pages and stuffed them in his pants pocket.

Reece pulled out some of the drawers. His search inside them didn't come up with anything of interest. He needed a better map. Next to the desk sat a stack of papers, scrolls, and wooden boxes of different sizes. He opened one box then another, realizing that the rectangular containers each held scrolls. One opened as he moved it, and he grasped the rolled-up parchment inside. It had drawings of land masses on a vine that was encircled within a globe.

"What are you doing?" The green Hobgoblin was taller than most. He reached just under Reece's chin. His back was a bit bent, and one leg dragged behind him. His thick ears were pointed with gray hairs spouting from his inner green ear.

"I —" Reece dropped the parchment — "was lost."

"Not likely. You are looking for something. If you think you will get out of here alive, you're wrong."

"Who will stop me?" Reece balled his fists.

The creature laughed. "You are human, and I am magical. There is no competition. I may seem like I have a weak leg, but I am still stronger than you." In a flash, the Hobgoblin was in front of Reece, a knife drawn and at Reece's neck.

Reece's nails started to grow, his teeth tingled, and his nose twitched. "Don't make assumptions." He whipped his hand forward and wrapped it around the Hobgoblin's neck. "I am looking for a garden. Tell me, do you know where it is?"

"I am not telling you —" the Hobgoblin coughed — "anything."

Tightening his grip, pushing his suggestion into the mind of the Hobgoblin, Reece felt the resistance, but with the strength he'd gained from his feeding, slicing through it was possible. "Tell me!"

"I don't know. You have to find it yourself. It's a secret garden. If I knew, it wouldn't be a secret."

The Hobgoblin's eyes watered as he fought the release of those words. His mind was struggling against the push of Reece's control.

"How, are you doing…"

"How do I get there?"

"The maps and clues will help you. Too many guards.

You will never make it past the throne room where it's likely to be…if you are visible." The creature struggled.

"Who is allowed in that area? The Soul Warriors? Any magicals?"

"Only the Beaniz dwarfs who eat the dust are allowed there. It is kept locked in case they find the girl's hybrid vamp-imp or her body."

Reece's hand twitched at the mention of Zamina. "I need a map. I will release you, but you will give me a map of this place."

"I can give you a map of only the entrance and just beyond the throne room. No one has entry or knowledge of the Overlord's personal sleeping quarters. His magic changes the location to keep his private area protected. It moves to a different side of the castle grounds at midnight when his magic is strongest."

"Where does his army meet? Who protects this place?"

The Hobgoblin's arms pushed against Reece's mental barrier. He grunted but couldn't move. "What are you?"

Reece smiled. "Just human. Isn't that what you see?"

The creature tried to move its head. "No, your eyes were brown. Now they're black like …no, her, the ah…" he grunted.

"Don't say her name. Why would you think I'm like her?"

"The eyes. No other creatures' eyes are so black that they suck you in – control you – but that of hers and the Vampires."

"Who protects this place?" Reece lifted him.

"Gargoyles, Berserkers, and Cyclops. The Soul Warriors will come when summoned. But the most powerful protection is the Overlord's power. The others are diversions until he is unleashed."

"You will forget me."

The Hobgoblin smiled. "I will not."

"What will happen if you disappear?"

"Disappear?"

"If you aren't here? Do you ever leave?"

"I do, sometimes for a few days to deliver goods to the training fields, the captain, or her second in command."

Reece called DewOfWinter. A gray mist formed in the middle of the room.

"The Mist Ones! They are not allowed here. They are not to be trusted with this information."

DewOfWinter materialized. "You summoned me?"

"Yes, can you take him away for a few days? Erase his memory?"

She smiled. "Gladly! And thank you for showing me the way into the Overlord's quarters. You, my master, have given me a gift I will repay."

"No! Get away from me!" The Hobgoblin struggled.

DewOfWinter returned to mist and wrapped herself around the Hobgoblin. Reece released the creature and ignored its muffled cry for help as he and DewOfWinter disappeared.

Reece exhaled, tired again, but turned to grab all the maps he could carry. Then he slipped into the floor and righted the rug back into place.

Chapter 24

Reece had been sneaking out every night after kissing Ora to sleep. It was starting to become even more addictive. He was finished with the array of weapons he'd designed and was bored while waiting for the others to finish their offerings for the Overlord. He hadn't told Ora about the maps he'd studied to memorize. He held back on revealing them to her as he explored as many places alone each night.

"Quiver, if you put that there, the weapon will jam." Reece tossed Quiver a screwdriver to help him pry the smaller blade from the handle of the axe he was working on.

"You're right. It doesn't need it."

"Are you almost done? I want to show you something I found."

Quiver wiggled the smaller blade from the base of the axe handle and then tossed it onto the large table they were working on. "It's hot in here with all the ovens going."

Reece shrugged. "It doesn't bother me."

"Nothing does. You aren't even breaking a sweat."

"I don't sweat much." He waved Quiver over to him. Reece dug into his pocket and removed an orange crystal he'd found while exploring one of the abandoned rooms in their wing the other night.

"What is this?" Power from the small crystal made it vibrate and jump in his hand.

"How did you get that? It's a stone from the Demi-god realm."

"Someone in the wing we were in had these."

"I wonder who they are working for, then. That's not something we would use or even could get."

Voices appeared and grew louder around them. Reece glanced over Quiver's shoulder. "The Overlord."

Reece stood straight. "Did you put your weapons on the table?" The Gnomes working with them moved about, quickly arranging each weapon.

"Everyone, I consider weaponry a valuable skill. Our army will be victorious because of what you have designed for them. By magic, I can replicate your creations, but without them, I cannot imagine how warriors of many shapes, sizes, and capabilities could use a weapon. I need you to stretch yourselves more. Design a weapon for the magical kind assigned to you."

"Your majesty, we have the recent creations available here." An older Gnome with a green and white streaked beard waved at the table.

"Interesting." The Overlord smiled. "But I want to know more about the creators of these weapons. If you create it, you should be able to wield it."

A hush dropped in the room. Reece couldn't believe the

Overlord was implying they would have to demonstrate.

"Sir, if I may, we have some delicate weaponsmiths here who may not be able to give a true demonstration of their creation…"

The Overlord held up a hand. "Then I don't want them creating my weapons." He walked over to Reece and tapped his finger on his chin. "The human may not survive."

Reece watched the Overlord's eyes glow, and the pressure to push into his thoughts felt physical. Inhaling slowly to calm his response, Reece willed himself not to push back but held firm. Cyrillus's lips thinned at the failed attempt.

"I will try to." Reece smiled.

"Good. You're first. Your, ah, katana against my guard here, who favors a battle axe."

Reece caught Ora's eye. She barely contained the concern on her face. Her lips were tight and her eyes wide. He'd have to play every move as an accidental win. Slowly, he walked over to the weapons table. He grasped the handle and glanced up at the Cyclops who beat his six feet four-inch frame by another three feet plus.

"I have one question."

Everyone who was whispering stopped.

"What? You want mercy?" Cyrillus had a lightness in his voice.

So, the Overlord thought he was a joke. That could work in his favor. "Yes, if he wins, will I still live?"

"This is not a game. We fight to the death. If your

143

weapon and skills are worthy, you will win."

"Then I can kill him," Reece spoke softly, lifting his eyes slowly up the form of the guard who'd taken his battle axe and tossed it from one hand to the other. The magicals around them spread out, making a giant circle.

"If you want to be considered the winner, you can try."

Reece cracked his neck to the side and slowly made his way to the middle of the circle. Everyone was quiet, not wanting to cheer or make a noise as they sensed they would be the next.

"Can I make one request?"

"Another question? What is it?"

"If I kill him, can you free the others from having to fight?"

Cyrillus turned and smiled at his guard. "No. If you want me to free the others, you'll have to kill both my guards."

A gasp echoed in the room.

"Your majesty"—the Gnome stepped forward—"he is a great talent. Is there not another you'd like to try first?"

"He may be a great talent, but he is hiding something. I can't read him, and something—" the Overlord sniffed— "smells unnatural about him."

"I beg you, sir, the magniton metal has arrived. The others have yet to be able to touch it. I've heard that he could."

"Then he better survive." The Overlord snapped his fingers, and his Cyclops guard charged forward.

Reece waited, bent until the last moment, and did a split as the axe swung at his head. He stabbed up into the groin of the Cyclops. Green blood sprayed from the wound. Reece lifted his katana to strike by pushing himself up, then into a backflip. His other hand was flung out straight to center him. The Cyclops threw his axe. Reece flexed his sword, knocking the axe off balance to avoid a slice at the head. He waited. The Cyclops growled and charged him again. Reece didn't move, giving the Cyclops a chance to get closer. He surged forward, slicing the magical down the chest. The Cyclops landed a blow to his chest. Reece was thrown by the force of it into the other magicals surrounding the fight. They pushed him back into the circle. The Cyclops grabbed him by the neck. The creature's hand was huge and squeezed tightly on Reece's throat.

"Die!"

Air was cut off. His head hurt. A crack vibrated through his ears as the bones in his neck broke. Reece allowed a surge of power to explode within him. He lifted his arm to slice the katana downward. The Cyclops dropped him. Reece landed on his knees, surging the sword under the Cyclops' ribs and straight through the heart. Snatching the blade out, he watched as green blood poured from the wound, and, with a thundering sound, the Cyclops fell to the floor.

The other guard charged, but Cyrillus held up a hand, stopping him immediately.

Reece stood with his eyes downcast, the sword at his side, heaving air in as he pushed the surge of power deep within and praying his incisors sank back within his mouth.

"Leave him!"

The others cheered.

His blood calmed, and Reece felt like himself again. He barely lifted his eyes to the Overlord. "Thank you." He bowed his head. Reece knew he needed to play a submissive role, the accidental winner of the fight.

"You better prove your worth, or you will fight me next time."

Reece didn't lift his head to look at the Overlord. He was afraid his eyes may have residue from the power surge.

He felt a slap on his back. "That was impressive!"

Reece let out a loud exhale and dropped his sword. "Uh! And exhausting." In more ways than one. While fighting the Cyclops, the Overlord had pressed hard on his mind to enter. The fight was a decoy, something to throw him off, to weaken his hold on the entrance to his thoughts. He fought both and won by holding power within himself. If it weren't for the necklace, he didn't know what he'd transform into. Reece knew he had to fight for more than closing off his thoughts from the Overlord. He needed to fight to hold onto what was left of his sanity.

Chapter 25

You lied to me?" Ora stood before him as she dropped one of the maps he'd shared onto the bed.

"I'm sorry, but I thought it was better to explore alone." Reece wiped his hand down his face. "Ora, I care about you." His voice broke, and at that moment, he thought maybe he more than cared about this girl who stole his heart, dulled his anger, and cured his grief.

"I don't believe you!" Tears fell from her eyes. "You played me for a fool." She turned from him to sob and wiped her eyes.

Reece went to her and placed his arm around her waist. "Please, Ora, forgive me for wanting you safe." He closed his eyes. "And hiding from you. I've made many mistakes, and there are things about me that I don't want you to know."

"Like, that you can kill without remorse?" She jerked away from him. "What was that today in the smithy?"

"Me saving my life and everyone else's."

"Something was different about you. I can't name it, but the energy around you felt different."

"Did others notice that, or was it just you who wasn't used to me when I fight?"

She turned to him. "I noticed. Reece, I've been watching you for over a year. The day we met at the race Megan has every year. I wanted you then, for myself, but Zamina always goes for what she wants. I knew I couldn't love a human or even a magical because my kind could kill any human or magical if they aren't strong enough to survive it when we mate."

"I taught you and Zamina how to fight at my parents' school. You've seen me spar."

Her hands flew up. "I've never seen you kill!"

"What was I supposed to do—let him kill me? The others?"

"No! I don't know. What is becoming of us? This war he wants... The creatures he is creating are all destruction to magicals and humans. I want this to be over. I want a happy life, but I don't know if that's for me. Kissing you made me make-believe, but even so, I could never be myself with you."

Reece stepped to her and pulled her into a kiss, closing his eyes as she allowed herself to give into the need for it. "You will be; one day, you can let go with me. I promise."

Ora pushed him away from her. "Don't make promises you can't keep."

"Let's deal with this between us later. I'd like you to come with me. I can show you everything. I've gotten far in the tunnels. I want to know what they are hiding in the lab area. I can find answers about Zamina. Make sure they aren't creating others like her, and uncover how we can permanently stop the Overlord and Megan from destroying our homes.

"Fine." Ora pivoted away from him and grabbed her knife and gloves. Then she adjusted her glasses and faced him. "I'm ready."

Reece waved her to follow and went to the closet. "You press here on the wall, on the small tear." He demonstrated, and the armoire moved, creating a slim opening to a tunnel several feet from the floor. "I'll go first. I know how to get there from studying the maps. Follow close behind me, but be really quiet. We don't want anyone to hear us – especially the mole people who built the tunnels."

"You saw them?"

"Yeah, once, but they went the other way." Reece fell silent as he went through the tunnel system he'd burned into his memory. Reece started to worry about it, making him search more aggressively for the garden. He'd made a few stops back to the warehouse storage room, thinking DewOfWinter may have dropped the shopkeeper back there, but she hadn't.

"What else were you able to find when you went alone?"

"Not much. Many of the rooms were empty. I went in each room, trying anything to locate the garden entrance painting I remember Zamina telling me about."

"Wouldn't her rooms be near the Overlord's?"

"No, they might be near the labs. If she needed someone to help her, in case she got sick."

"How are you able to see in this dark tunnel?"

"I memorized the maps."

"Yes, but you didn't the first time."

"I felt my way around until I saw the light." It was partially true. He hated avoiding the truth this way. Telling her about himself too soon could ruin everything. She'd try to kill him, and he would stop her, then he'd be alone. Reece wasn't ready to be alone again. That day would come soon enough.

"Just a little bit farther."

This part of the tunnel had an incline that could be considered stairs but was worn and chipped rock. They had to maneuver up several feet to get to a level tunnel. The lab floor was above them. An indentation in the rock had a small protrusion.

"You ready?" He slid the trapdoor open. Like the other rooms where the entrance was on the floor, a rug was in place. The room was dark, so Reece wanted to believe there would be no one guarding it or walking around. Tentatively, he moved the rug aside. Then he pushed his head up from the floor. There were floor-to-ceiling structures on each wall. A light blue glow emanated from them. He couldn't see what was on the designs, except they were trimmed in bronze and broken red crystals were embedded within the case.

Reece climbed up and out of the hole then reached down to help Ora. They stood and waited, making sure they were alone. It was extremely silent, except for an occasional beep.

Ora gave Reece a nod then stepped forward. He followed, his muscles tight. He turned to see the wall bore a massive picture of a garden maze.

"The painting." Reece reached out and grabbed Ora's upper arm. "It is of a garden."

She stopped and turned. They walked toward the painting. It was not bright and green like he would expect a garden to be, but the pictures of the scattered clusters of bushes were thorned. The flowers had teeth, and there were vine walls, statues, and scattered statues of different species of magicals at each turn.

"We need to take this or memorize it. This statue, the Griffin, is the exit to the forest where I met Zamina."

"I can trace to see if she'd been here before." Ora removed her glasses and touched the painting. Her eyes, bronze and blue, glowed. Her nose flared. Her hand jerked away.

"Did you get anything?"

"Yes, and it's not good."

"Tell me."

"She was here, but she wasn't alone. Someone was following her and came here soon after she arrived."

"Who?"

"A Soul Thief, the one who brought us in and sent the other back. He knows something. It doesn't make sense why he would be tracking her here when she was free to roam this place."

"Maybe she wasn't supposed to be in here."

"We have to be careful of him."

"I don't think this is the lab—" Reece cursed— "they

don't label anything on those maps."

"It's got to be important." She pointed at a door on the side wall. "That's a magically enhanced lock on the door."

Reece noticed the door glowed green and had no knob for an exit. "How's anyone supposed to get out of here?"

"Their essence has to be recognized by the door."

"What's in here that they need to protect?" Reece turned away from the painting to walk toward the enclosures from floor to ceiling with copper and jeweled sides. The flow from the front of the enclosures danced on the floor. Reece stepped in front of one, and his jaw dropped.

The tall structure held one-man red hair and green eyes. His body was suspended in a gel substance that was translucent with streaks of black. Reece stepped back from it.

"He looks just like…" Reece narrowed his gaze at the floating man.

"Megan."

Reece walked down the row that contained more magicals trapped in similar cases. All floated in suspended sleep. "What is wrong with them? Are they dead?"

"No, I've heard rumors but never imagined it was true." Ora came to stand next to Reece. "They are Sandmen. Their essence is bound to the Overlord's, and he makes them gather information or punish beings through their dreams or nightmares."

"How can we get them out?"

"We can't. The magic holding them is dark magic. The

gel… will burn through us. It's like a bomb. The only one who can free them is the one who put them there."

Reece heard a crack and then the echo of a pop. He lifted his hand. Ora pulled out her knife and crept alongside him. A spider, about six feet tall, had the torso and face of a woman and black, almond-shaped eyes that widened. Her upper arms were human, but the lower six were of a spider. She hissed at them and sprang.

Ora threw her knife into its stomach. Reece kicked it, striking it between its eyes. The spider flew into one of the cases, smashing its back against it, and slid down to the floor. She let out a loud squeal.

"Shut her up!" Reece charged at her.

Ora ripped off her glasses and jerked up her hand. With a twist, the spider's mouth was sealed closed. The spider rose and stumbled back.

Reece jumped on its stomach and grabbed it by the neck. With its clawed black nails, the creature's hand scratched at his arms. "We must get rid of her, or she might tell others we were here."

"If we do, they'll see the body."

"Maybe not." Reece summoned DewOfWinter.

A mist formed from the ceiling and dripped down to the floor. DewOfWinter transformed from the fog with a smile. "You called?"

"Can you take the spider?" Reece held the struggling creature in a chokehold.

"Gladly. DewOfWinter turned around. Where are we?"

"How did she get here?" Ora sat on the spider's stomach and pushed down two middle legs with her knees.

"I'll tell you later." Reece adjusted his arm on the spider's neck. "On three, let go so DewOfWinter can take the spider."

DewOfWinter clapped. "I'm ready."

Chapter 26

Reece was at his table when Wykwor dropped the magniton at his feet. It sounded like music when it hit the floor. Reece released the hammer he was holding and stretched to pick up the cloth sack of metal.

"The Overlord wants you to create a breastplate and weapon his beast can wield as well as in his human appearance."

Reece frowned. "His beast?"

"Yes, you do know the Overlord is a shapeshifter?"

"I heard he was. Is he a lion shifter or werewolf?"

Wykwor shook his head. "Never-ever say the word werewolf around him. He is unique in that he created his own beast, unlike any other known to man or magical. It's what makes him special and unlike any king before him."

"So, how can I design a weapon for a beast I haven't seen?" Reece honestly didn't want to see what the Overlord turned into. He only wanted to get the answers he'd come to this place for.

"That will be arranged."

"I will need help to create this. Can Quiver work with me?"

"If you require it, he can." Wykwor added, "I will make the guards and fellow Gnomes aware of it. Make sure Quiver knows that, if he works with you, he also will have to be presented to the Overlord when the weapons are done."

Reece waited until Wykwor left and waved Quiver over. The other magicals working on their weapons stopped and observed them before coming over to watch Reece take the metal out of the bag.

"It will burn ye if ye are not of its choosing." The Minotaur with a horse's body pointed at the sack.

"Let's see." Reece grabbed the sack's handles and lifted it onto the table.

"Every piece chooses," Quiver added. "So, you may be able to pick up one, but not another."

"Well, that one didn't like me." Reece reached for one of the larger pieces and grasped it. It vibrated, heated up, and flung itself across the room. He flicked his hand against the burn from the metal.

The others around him whispered, "Keep trying."

Quiver pointed to the bag. Reece hoped the change in him since being bitten by Zamina didn't make him unable to work with the metal. If that happened, he wouldn't last long here.

He picked up another piece of the multi-colored metal. It did the same. The other weapon smiths watched as he opened the sack further. He realized the patterns on the metals with red in them were the ones he'd touched that rebelled against him. He searched for metals with the same design he'd shaped before. Instead of touching the others with his hand, he moved them out of the way with a cloth from the sack.

"This one." Reece reached in and touched the magniton that bore the same patterns of colors as the one from the sword and blade he'd created before. It didn't move. He smiled and wrapped his hand around the thick piece.

The others cheered.

"You did it!" Quiver patted Reece on the back.

A male with straight white hair, purple eyes, and his mouth covered from his nose to chin in a green gauze-like wrapping waved one of the pieces of magniton that repelled from Reece. "Can I take these?"

Reece lifted an eyebrow. "What's your name?

"Unoi, Demi-god bastard, at your service." He bowed. "Thanks for fighting for the rest of us."

"Yeah, sure." Reece reached to shake hands. Unoi lifted his dark purple-nailed hand in a fist. Reece touched fists with him.

Unoi shrugged. "My palm has eyes in it. They don't like it when someone puts their hands over them."

"Oh, got it. Do you want to work over here with us? I have some tools I made myself that I've used before with this type of metal. They make it easier and better that we don't handle the metal as much."

"Okay, I'd like that. Those Ogre smell – bad. Real bad." Unoi went to his area to gather his things.

"You think he's the one who dropped the orange

crystal?" Quiver whispered.

"I hope so. I have questions for him."

"Everyone! Get to your stations. The Overlord is coming."

The crowd scattered, leaving Quiver and Reece with the sack sitting open. Reece quickly grabbed the other pieces of metal that matched the pattern he needed and closed the sack. He pushed the bag aside as the Overlord and his guard walked into the room.

The Overlord crossed his arms. "Well, it appears everyone is making progress."

Reece felt the gentle pressure of the constant attempt to break into his thoughts. It was the strongest he'd felt from anyone. He smiled and watched the Overlord slowly walk down the weapons table.

"I need to see who could touch the magniton. I will have a moment scheduled to speak to each of you."

Fighting against the urge to look at Unoi, Reece stepped forward. "I have touched it."

The Overlord nodded at him. "Anyone else?"

No one responded. Unoi remained silent. Reece forced his expression to remain placid.

"Very well. You." The Overlord tilted his head in Reece's direction. "Finish up tonight, but tomorrow, your day will be in my wing, drawing out the design for the weapon and breastplate. You will be moved there to complete your work if I conquer."

One step closer to finding the Garden entrance, Reece

bowed slightly and remained silent until the Overlord left. Quiver came over to Reece and whispered, "Why didn't the guy speak up?"

"I don't know. Can you find out? We'll talk more tonight." Reece didn't want to consider why Unoi had concealed his ability to touch the magniton. He knew it was because the magical was keeping it for himself. Reece thought he could do the same. Create a blade for himself while making the weapon for the Overlord.

Chapter 27

A re you ready to tell me everything?" Ora paced the room. She was still dressed in her soft leather pants, short boots, and long-sleeved shirt from earlier in the day.

"This guy Unoi—he said he was a Demi-god—could touch some of the magniton. He didn't reveal that fact to anyone but Quiver and me."

"Doesn't make sense. He's got to be working for someone not in the Vigilant."

"Maybe he is trying to escape. We are prisoners here."

"The Mist Ones? How did she show up when we were in that room filled with Sandmen? Remember, the Mist Ones were banned by the Overlord's magic and couldn't find this place."

"They can now." Reece shrugged. "I met her when I left you in the beginning, and she took me to the workhouse. Ever since then, we've had a connection."

"This can be an advantage, even a way out and back into the Overlord's castle. The Mist Ones can be our allies. Strangely, a human and a Mist One can communicate."

"I guess. I always could communicate mentally with my

twin sister."

"Quiver is coming in to go with us this time. I am still determining what will happen after I meet with the Overlord alone. He's been trying to probe my thoughts, get into my head."

She frowned. "And you can keep him out? A human?"

Reece knew he had to tell her the truth. He didn't want to; it would change everything between them. He stepped up to her and put his hand on her waist.

"Ora, how do you feel about me?" Reece studied her reaction.

"I care about you, but I can't allow myself to feel more than that for you. It's futile and would cause me too much pain. I've lost the only other person I allowed myself to care about. I won't do that again."

Reece didn't want to reveal too much now that Ora mentioned her guilt and torment with having to destroy Zamina. "I am human but have some abilities I use to protect myself."

"Have you always had them? These abilities?" Ora frowned, her eyes and essence filling with suspicion.

"Some of them have always been within me. Others, I'm discovering the more I am here. Some part of me knows what I can do, but my mind hasn't accepted it."

"You are dealing with magicals. The Overlord's magic keeps this universe alive. He is just that powerful. Don't try to use whatever abilities you think you have against him. He will kill you and rip the soul from you and use it as a source to siphon dark magic from the fallen angels trapped in the abyss."

"I won't. I only use what I must to protect my thoughts from him."

"If we get separated, how will I find you?"

"I will find you; don't worry. Tonight, we need to find the lab."

"Okay, that may give us some answers."

"One more thing before Quiver gets here." Reece stepped in closer. "Can I —"

"Kiss me." Ora leaned in, pressed her body to his, and pulled him into a kiss.

Reece inhaled the essence of her magic and grew drunk on it. She opened her mouth under the persuasive tilt of his lips. Her sweet combination of the human and unique taste of magic flooded his senses. With each delve deeper into her luscious lips, he drew more and more of her strength. He wondered, dreamed of when he could take things further, touch her full figure like he wanted. Reece closed his eyes against that desire; it was dangerous.

There was a knock on the door. Reece released Ora, noting that she stumbled a bit. Her lips were full, swollen from their kisses. She was breathless but smiled through it at him.

"You take my breath away." She fell back in the chair and closed her eyes while she yawned. "Which is impossible. How are you able to kiss me? I was told my kiss would kill a human man and suck all of the magic out of a magical. I wonder if the warnings are untrue."

"Maybe, but don't get sleepy on me. I don't want to go alone with Quiver." Reece went to the door and opened it.

She giggled and stood. "I am not sleepy." She adjusted her glasses.

Quiver rushed into the room. "Oh, yours is nicer than mine. You have a couch and a king-sized bed?" He turned. "A walk-in closet? Wow!"

"We picked this room instead of staying in one of the others."

"So, you are sleeping in here – together?" Quiver raised an eyebrow.

"I have to guard him. He tries to escape a lot."

"Sure." Quiver smirked.

"We will try to get information on the virus attacking the shifters and find out what creations they are splicing for this war the Overlord is preparing to start."

"I'm ready."

"Did you talk to that guy Unoi?"

"I did, and he told me to mind my business, or he would sneak into my room and kill me in my sleep."

"He said that?"

"Yep, without a blink of his eye."

"Try to make him your friend. Get him to trust you. We may need his help."

"That's not easy, but I can make it happen."

"I've made something for myself." Reece took a dagger

he had made from his pocket. "It's not as refined as the one the Overlord took from me, but it will do the job if we need it."

"Wait. I didn't bring a weapon. Am I going to need one?" Quiver put his hand up in front of him.

"I've got something you can use." Ora handed Quiver a *bo-shuriken* shaped like a star that could be hidden. "Throw it at the opponent, but make it count."

"Got it."

"Let's go." Reece led them into the tunnels. They moved quietly in the darkness. The smell was stale, but Reece inhaled deeper. Something was in the tunnels with them.

"Moles!" Quiver growled.

"Only a little further," Reece whispered. Then he stopped. The scratching of long nails echoed through the tunnels. The vibration of teeth chomping made Reece narrow his eyes to see what was coming.

"Let me go ahead of you." Quiver moved next to Reece. "I'll take care of it. You both go to the lab; I'll catch up."

"But the body. We can't leave any clues behind."

Quiver growled. His eyes glowed gold, and his teeth elongated. "I'll be sure to finish every bite."

Reece grabbed Ora's hand, and they went around Quiver, who was turning into a leopard three times his normal size. Quiver's beast had a gold coat that seemed to shimmer with a light of its own and black spots that moved at a hypnotic rock with his muscles. His body was tight within the tunnels.

"Let's go before you fall under a spell." Ora pulled him into the opening of the door then opened it. Reece stumbled behind her, his eyes adjusting to the darkness.

Quiver's beast, striking with snakelike speed, ripped into the neck of the huge mole that came around the corner.

Chapter 28

They stepped through the doorway, inside a closet full of lab coats, and closed the door. Blankets and pillows hung on a rack above them. They heard movement outside of the cabinet and faint talking. Reece used his ability to communicate with Ora without talking. He didn't want to risk them being found. *Do you want to attack or wait?*

He swallowed. If he attacked, she'd see what he was. If they waited, he could hide the ugly truth longer. No matter what, he needed answers on what DNA was used to create Zamina. The knowledge would help him know who he was and why he didn't die or turn back to normal when she was killed.

Ora took a moment to respond. Wait. Move slowly. See who is there.

Reece slowly slid the door to the open closet inch by inch until he could see outside. Ora tapped his shoulder, motioning to switch places with him. He moved out of the way, and she settled into the area, bending down and taking off her glasses. She tucked them into her pocket as her eyes glowed, releasing a stream of bluish magic.

Reece watched and listened as Ora exuded her power over those in the room. Sniffing in the essence of her magic, he was surprised at how quickly she recovered from his extraction of her magic earlier. He'd taken enough to cause her fatigue, but she'd replenished more rapidly.

The voices quieted. He heard a few thumps as bodies landed on the floor. Ora opened the door. Light from the lab flooded inside the closet. Reece followed Ora into the room. He turned in a circle, shocked to see cages of magicals slumped in a deep sleep. Reece and Ora stepped around the people in lab coats lying on the floor. Reece scented them and realized they were shifters of different species of animals.

They quietly walked through the rows of cages. There were Elves, a Unicorn, some Faeries, a Goblin, and a Hydra with nine heads, all serpents. In the last few cages, Reece stopped Ora. He pointed. There were children. Eight of them. They looked human but had grey skin and black eyes. They weren't in a cage; they were in a thick glass box.

"What are they?"

"Zamina's siblings. The failed experiments." Ora walked over to the fallen lab aide. She picked up the notepad the scientist was scribbling on before Ora's spell caused her to fall asleep.

"What are they doing?" Reece watched as they gathered the glass, scratched at it, and placed their hands on it. One started sinking into a black puddle that formed at its feet. The others just watched. The one child wholly submerged in the inky black goo disappeared, but the goo remained. The black tar puddle moved side to side on the box floor then climbed up to the top as though searching for a way out.

"It is trying to get to you?" Ora frowned. "That's strange.

They only do that for a victim or for Zamina."

"How do you know?"

"She told me about them. She missed them, of course; they were all she had inside the lab."

"No, she had a boy."

"He was created by the same scientist, but he wasn't nice to her at all."

"Where's the computer system?" Reece looked around then spied a rolling desk with a laptop. "How long will they be sleeping?"

"I don't know. My poison works differently on each magical species."

Reece walked to the laptop and smiled. "It's still open, unlocked. The scientist must have been working in it when you knocked her out." He pecked through the keys, searching for anything that could tell him about Zamina.

"What are you looking for? I may be able to pull her thoughts out to get information."

"What combination did they use to create Zamina and, uh, her siblings? Did they create another like her?"

"Okay." Ora's eyes started to glow green, and the magic from them rolled down her arm to the hand she'd placed on the fallen scientist.

Reece found files of pictures of two magicals and lines connecting some of their features to a table with labels: Extracted, Transformed, Subject. He searched the database for Subject, typing in Zamina's name.

Her name came up. Next to it were two names: Afanas, a Succubi, and Cyrillus.

Reece pushed the computer aside.

"What did it say?"

"Afanas? And Cyrillus."

"The Vampire king? That's a strong blood curse and the Overlord – can't imagine how she got a sample of his DNA."

"How did they get blood from Afanas? They must have tricked him into giving it."

Reece read the notes. "It says that Afanas' blood was tainted when they used it; he had some illness. That's what made Zamina different. The virus the Vampire had in its blood at the time of the infusion to the embryo allowed the attachment of the DNA to repair Zamina. They believe the Succubi blood and that of the Overlord created the virus that afflicted the shifters. They added Afanas' DNA after they realized she was infecting shifters."

"Is there any more of his blood?" Ora approached Reece.

He read quickly then clicked through several of the files. "They said they used all of it on her. But look"—he pointed— "They are trying to do the experiment again."

A yell vibrated the room around them. One of the scientists woke. Its blue eyes grew, and it sprouted black hair, long teeth, and a horn as it fell onto all fours. An Ogre rounded the corner with a battle club and charged at Ora.

She threw a knife, hitting it in one eye, but it didn't stop. The scientist turned into a large black puma. Its eyes glowed, and its teeth elongated. It leaped over the Ogre and on top of Reece. Reece wrestled with the beast as it bit his arm. The creature started to gag and spit green blood. Reece kicked up, but the beast bit into his shoulder. A heat Reece wasn't prepared for a burst from his stomach. His nails grew, his incisors protruded, and the power he'd held at bay rushed from him. Twisting, he flipped over the puma shifter, sat on its stomach, then pressed his hands inside its mouth, ripping its jaws open. Unable to help himself, he bit down into its chest, sucking blood and magic into his throat. The rush of it was delicious and fed him strength and power beyond anything he'd felt since he bit his twin sister.

"Reece! What are you doing?"

He felt a hand on his shoulder and heard the roar of Quiver as his beast attacked another wakened scientist.

Ora kicked him off the shifter, who'd turned back into its human form. Reece stood. Blood from the scientist was splattered all over his clothes and hands. He raised his eyes to Ora's and saw terror there deep within.

"Ora—" He stepped forward. She stepped back. "I'm not..."

"Don't say it! You lied! You liar." Shaking, she ran to the closet, leaving him and Quiver in the lab.

Quiver transformed into his human, making it a point to snatch a lab coat and put it on before turning around.

"So, she's ticked."

"Yeah, we need to get out of here, but I can't leave this lab intact."

"Nope, other guards are coming. I hear them."

"Give me the orange stone." Quiver extended his hand.

Reece reached into his pocket and handed it to him. "What are you using it for?"

"To clean up our mess. Go into the tunnels. I'm following you."

"You sure?"

"Yeah, hurry up. Go find Ora. I'll fix this."

Reece nodded. "Thanks." He ran into the closet and through the tunnel. He'd only made it a few yards when he heard the explosion. Rocks in the tunnel were falling, but the structure held. Reece hurried to his room. Ora wasn't there. He went to the shower and washed the blood off his body. Then he tossed the clothes into the fireplace. Tightening the towel around his waist, he started the fire.

He'd screwed up, bad. Ora was gone, likely to consider killing him for lying to her and being a vampire.

"Hey? Where is Ora?"

Reece turned around. "Gone. I don't know."

Quiver had grabbed a pair of jeans and a button-down black shirt from the closet. "Well, neither of us saw that coming. You didn't give off the scent of death like most vamps." He sniffed the air. "A sour smell just under the scent of blood and something...that smells sweet, divine, fresh."

"I'm a mixture of many things. Vampire, and my sister, she'd been given a gift by an angel, I nearly drank her dry, and that angel's gift transferred to me, saving some of my human blood and qualities with it."

"That's something that should never have happened.

You shouldn't have survived any of that."

"I know, but it's more complicated. I also survived wearing a Soul Trainer's ring my brother had on him."

"How did you get it off? I heard they don't come off once they are on while the Soul Warrior is alive. The Soul Thieves have the ring, and the female Soul Trainers have the necklace."

"I took it off before it attached to me, I guess."

"You camouflage well as a human."

"I need to. If I don't, Cyrillus will kill me or worse."

"Don't worry. The Vigilant kept you alive for a reason. I'll make sure you stay alive."

"Are you sure? I mean, Zamina was the one who started the virus that's taking down the shifters. I don't know if I have the same affliction."

"You bit that shifter scientist, and he didn't get the virus."

"How do you know?"

"I've seen it, and it infects quickly. Dead or alive, every shifter turns into a cannibalistic zombie. That didn't happen."

"Thanks for telling me. He was my first bite in a long time."

"You don't need blood to survive?"

"No, I can eat food for substance. It tastes horrible, though. I can be satisfied stealing exposed magic from magicals."

Quiver's eyes widened. "You took some of my magic, didn't you? It's why I was always sleepy after working with you."

Reece shrugged. "Sorry."

"Low, real low to steal someone's magic."

"I didn't steal so much as take what you let escape."

"Whatever. Still a low blow."

"Okay, maybe it was. Want me to ask next time?" Reece smiled.

"No need. I don't want the hassle of trying to hold my magic in. Take what you need of it."

"What happened to the lab? What do you think the Overlord will do about it?"

"He'll look for whoever destroyed the place."

"How will he know?"

"Well, maybe he will start with the remnants of the orange crystal I left behind." Quiver smiled.

"Thanks for taking care of things." Reece placed a hand on Quiver's shoulder.

"Anytime." Quiver opened the door then left the room.

Reece reached out in his mind, searching for Ora's. Nothing. She'd blocked him out. He couldn't blame her; the look on her face was shattering.

Chapter 29

Being in the Overlord's presence was unsettling and exhausting. Reece wanted to leave but had been invited to the Overlord's private wing before he could get to work on any of the weapons the leader requested. He still had his partially finished dagger hidden under the skin of his shin.

The library they were in was extensive, fit for a giant with small and large books as tall as Reece stood. High-backed chairs, reading areas with comfortable couches for giants, and average-sized magicals were situated in strategic places where the light from the moon or sun reflected inside. There were even game tables set up. The smell of books, worn paper, and dust filled the room.

"Do you like to read?" the Overlord asked as he sat beside Reece. His guard and an additional Berserker with yellowed teeth and sharp nails paced the room near the door.

"I do, but haven't done much since, well...coming here." Reece searched the room for possible exits.

"What did you read?"

"History, ancient and especially about weapons." "Why would you want to start a war with humans if you have all of this?" Reece took a few deep breaths to push the pressure

Cyrillus imposed in his mind to find a crack in his defenses.

Cyrillus smiled. "The war I would impose already happened with my ancestors. They are prisoners of war, and you humans, well…because of you, it happened."

"Your ancestors' problems aren't yours. You know we call them demons. They are trapped in an abyss. If you cross over, that could be you. There is a higher power who controls the rules."

"I suppose, but I am willing to take my chances."

"For what—revenge against your dead wife? That's what it sounds like to me."

Reece felt a sharp punch in his mind and reared back from the unexpected blow. His head hurt – bad, but he wouldn't give Cyrillus any pleasure in the assault by revealing it.

"Perceptive. That isn't my only reason. The population of magicals is growing beyond what I can handle with my magic. Holding The Void together takes more of my energy, strength, and resources than I'd like."

"Isn't that why you are supposed to have a queen? You and she would share the burden and work together. Maybe you should just find a new wife." Reece shrugged.

The Overlord chuckled. "I don't want another wife. I loved only one woman, and she betrayed my interest for her own."

"What about an heir? Don't you want kids? All kings have to have an heir."

Reece frowned at the thin-set lips and angry eyes

reflecting back at him.

"My former wife was pregnant when she died at my hand, and she cursed me. I cannot bear children, even though I have tried through natural means. I will rule until I cannot."

"As a human, what is my reason for being here? Magicals in the weapons smithy take me as a joke?"

"Humans are here for several reasons. There are half-breeds who don't quite fit in on the Earthen Realm and have muted magic because they are there. Some, like you, have a special talent we desire. Others have a tie here, either from a former Soul Warrior parent or a protégé of Merlin who comes here to steal our magic while creating pathways for magicals to break into the human world."

"If I create the weapons you want, will you set me free?"

The Overlord smirked. "Well, that depends. If we win the war, of course."

"Can you tell me about the crystals and what they are for? I don't usually put them in my weapons so I need to know what kind does what."

"Well, it is a conduit for magic. Some of them even have magical properties and energies within them."

"Does your magic come from crystals?"

"No, I was born of natural magic. It's hard to explain, but there is a difference between the procreation of a magical species and a new, never-before-created magical. The magic created by the fallen ones to create magical creatures, then, without further manipulations, some are created spontaneously through magic. I am the result of a new magical as I shift into many forms and can decide on my dominant shifter form."

"Would your children have that ability?"

"No, it's not likely. They will pull their likeness from my parents, who were a specific species of magicals."

"Oh, I think I understand. So, the crystals you want in your breastplate and in the handle of your weapon? What do you want them to be able to do?"

"They will increase my power and abilities, taking some of the management and distribution of magic off my shoulders during battle. My magic has to be balanced to hold The Void together, or realms suffer, and magicals die."

"Oh, then I will make sure to do a good job creating them for you."

"Make sure you do, Cade Abara, if that is your true name."

"If it's alright with you, sir, can I get back to work?" Reece stood.

"Of course, I'll have one of my guards take you." The Overlord crossed his legs in the chair. "But one more thing. You should see my beast so you know how to fashion the weapon to work with my human and beast forms."

Reece swallowed; he didn't want to see the Overlord in beast form but had no choice as the man before him started to transform. The Overlord's face elongated; his hair waved into an orange flame from the roots to the tips. The skin on his face pulled back as the bone within it extended, widened, and grew. Cyrillus's body exploded with muscle and bone that expanded him at least another six feet. What emerged was a colossal beast with brick red hair, a face of white bone full of jagged teeth, and a sharp claw on his front and hind legs. Its eyes were fathomless black. Regally, it bent down to face Reece. A chill pumped through Reece's blood. He was staring at pure evil.

"This is my favorite form, although I can take many. Build your weapons to fit in my claws or mouth."

Reece shivered because, within those black eyes, he saw death.

Chapter 30

The room was dark, cold, and quiet without Ora in it. Reece was sprawled back in the oversized chair in the corner. He was calming his blood from the long day with the Overlord. He was mentally and physically exhausted. A knock sounded on the door. Reece dragged himself up and opened it.

Quiver stood there with a goofy smile. "Guess what?"

"Really? I don't have time for games."

"I recruited him." Quiver waved at someone.

Reece leaned out of the doorway and saw Unoi walking up the hall. He didn't have the energy to smile but opened the door wider and sat back in the chair next to the fireplace.

"Nice room."

"I know, right?" Quiver elbowed Unoi.

"So, what happened while I was with the Overlord?"

"All hell broke loose. The fire in the lab caused a stir. The guards shook us all down to see if we knew anyone who could be involved."

"Oh?" Reece leaned up. "Did they find any clues?"

"Not yet. They can't get into the room. Someone set off

a bomb that just so happened to cause a ton of rubbish to block the tunnel entrances and the doors." Quiver cleared his throat. "So, we have a problem. Because of the crystal I used to cause the explosion, I left some evidence behind to point to a Demi-god's involvement."

"And?" Reece stood up, noticing Quiver was pacing, and Unoi was standing there with his eyebrows raised as it dawned on him that Quiver had implicated him in a crime.

"You framed me?!" He pushed Quiver in the chest.

Reece stood between them. "He did frame you. But we can fix it."

"We can?" Quiver's mouth dropped.

"I can. I have a friend who can pop in there and get rid of the evidence."

Unoi tilted his head to the side. "You are human, right? So, who do you know that can do that?"

"I'm, yeah, human and something else. But it doesn't matter." Reece held a hand at Quiver to warn him to keep his secret. "Just wait a minute." He summoned DewOfWinter. Within moments the ceiling of the room was filled with mist, which grew dense as it dripped from the wall. Her feet formed first, then her ballooned sheer pants, tanned belly button adorned with jewelry, and her arms.

"Yes?" she asked, as her head seemed to pop from the ceiling.

"Hi, DewOfWinter, I have a problem. I would like you to go to the lab with Quiver to get something.

"Of course, but master, I have a request."

"You don't have to call me master. I am not your master." Reece sighed and smoothed his hair behind his ears.

"You call me, and I am certainly compelled to come, to answer against my own will, no matter what I am doing. So, stop controlling me if you don't want me to call you that."

"I don't want to control you. I need your help. Are you willing to keep giving it?"

She tapped her foot while the others stared at her with shocked expressions.

"Yes, we are working for the same cause. The Overlord has imprisoned my people, kept them out of his castle, and destroyed our homes, so we have no choice but to serve him. Our mist forms are tethered and hover above the mote surrounding his properties. We've ruled the space above the clouds, and he has poisoned them with his dark magic."

"Can you bring others here if we need you to?" Reece stepped forward. "Like Ashti? Your king?"

DewOfWinter laughed. "He is in hiding with his love. I would not bring him into this. My sisters and I can manage the onslaught when you are ready." She smiled.

"Wait?" Quiver elbowed Reece. "You – are – working with the Mist Ones?"

"I'm impressed." Unoi patted Reece on the back. "For a human, you may actually help the cause."

"Really? Who are you working for, Unoi?"

Unoi smiled. "A red-haired she-devil sent me to spy on you."

"Megan?!"

"Megan?" DewOfWinter asked. "The daughter of the missing, dearly departed Rumpelstiltskin?"

"She is alive and well on her mission to stop our insane leader from opening the doors of hell for all of us." Unoi snorted.

"I think her father is alive." Reece tapped his chin. "I saw him and others in cases, floating, some dark magic holding them in place. Their eyes were open, never blinking. I think they are called Sandmen."

"Show me them." DewOfWinter stomped.

"I will after you help Quiver. We don't have a lot of time."

"Alright, come with me." She transformed into mist and wrapped herself around Quiver and Unoi. They all disappeared.

Reece pressed his mind forward again. Imagining Ora, seeing where she was, and realizing she wasn't resisting. She was in the room next door. He got up.

"I'm going to talk to her even if she doesn't want to hear what I have to say." He opened the door to find Ora standing there.

"Hi, I was coming for you." Reece reached out and touched her arm. He stood still, waiting for her to jerk away. She didn't immediately but edged by him. Reece didn't move; he closed his eyes as her hip touched his.

"You are a vampire." She pivoted and faced him as he closed the door. "She changed you, and you've been feeding off me since we met. I don't know how because Zamina needed to bite to feed and could only take my magic if I controlled the giving of it without biting."

"I'm different. I can't explain it except that I accidentally mixed her vampire change with an angel's gift and maybe even a Soul Thief's ring."

"That's not possible." She crossed her arms.

"Trust me on it. That's completely possible. One night, my sister came to my room, glowing from a run-in with an angel. I was in the middle of a change, and I nearly drained her, but she came to with the strength of ten men and kicked me off her. By that time, I was glowing but still a vampire."

"You could start another virus." She straightened her back.

"Not possible. I don't need to feed on magic or blood to survive. The angelic gift kept part of me human. Food will sustain me, but magic and blood strengthen me and taste much better."

"So, what? I was a dessert to you?" Ora shook her head and moved back.

"No." Reece moved close to her. "You were life to me. I know this is not the right time, and I'm not what you would want. I feel so strongly for you, and it's not lust or manipulation like I felt with Zamina. With you, this is a complicated feeling, one I can't shake that has nothing to do with magic. It has to do with you and me at this moment, and still, I can connect with you like I haven't to anyone."

"I don't believe it. Do you even know why I kissed you back?"

"I hope because you like me too."

Ora sighed. "Because anyone else magical or human who kisses me is seduced by the magic I have. You didn't act that way and didn't die from it. I tested you, and each time we kissed gave you more and more of my magic, and you ate it up. I didn't understand how a human could not be affected by my magic. I was starting to think I could return to the Earthen Realm after all this. Now, I know that's not possible."

"So, I was an experiment to you?" The thought really hurt, and Reece stepped closer, wanting to dare her to prove it.

She lifted her chin. "You said it. I didn't."

"Then you may as well feel the fullness of me." Reece picked her up by her waist and backed her into the wall. Before she could argue, he pressed his body against hers and kissed her deeply.

She didn't even struggle. Ora kissed him back. The power of her kiss made his entire body tingle. She was warm, then hotter, making his cold body friendly and his human blood pump through his body. He felt like his old self but so much stronger for a moment. He kissed her like he was starving, and she returned that kiss with as much vigor as he gave.

Someone cleared his throat.

"Did we interrupt something?" Quiver chuckled.

Reece jumped away from Ora and shook his head to right the drunken haze over him. He felt as though he was ten times stronger than ever before. Reece put his hand to his head.

"We were testing something."

Unoi cleared his throat. "Yeah, right."

Reece touched Ora's shoulder. "She's helping by feeding me."

Quiver raised an eyebrow. "Well, we got the evidence, but we have a problem."

"What?"

"Megan, Unoi said you had a bracelet that gave her a signal to you being here?"

"Yeah, but I broke it."

Unoi waved his hand. "She locked in on you. That's how I got here. Megan has friends everywhere, and her attack on the castle will come as soon as she gathers her forces."

"That's not good. The Overlord hates her and blames her for standing in his way."

Ora walked over to the fireplace. "I think he also is imprisoning her father as a Sandman. She thinks he killed her father. I'm sure that's why she really wants to attack him. Wait until she finds out he's been alive and enslaved as a dream walker all these years. They will tear this place apart for all of us."

"We can't let that happen. The Demi-god realm has suffered enough from his pulling of magic from our realm to pour it into resources for his war. If he knows we are going against him, he may destroy our realm, but there is nothing we can do since he is slowly killing us anyway."

"He is not supposed to rule alone. Without a queen he can balance the magic with; eventually, all the realms will suffer." Quiver leaned on the dresser.

"Then we have to split up. There is a pendant that the queen wears. If we get that, it can bind Megan's magic to the Overlord's. They are the most powerful beings here in The Void. Their magic can balance the realms. If we can call Megan by her name, weaken her Rumpelstiltskin magic long enough to put the pendant on her."

"What does binding their magic mean?" Reece asked.

"It means they can't get rid of each other. They are completely in sync with each other, whether they want to be or not. It's a constant push and pull of their magic; they have to give and take. It can be torture if you aren't in love with the person."

Reece felt Ora's eyes on him. Did she think that way about him — because Reece felt the pull of magic to his?

Chapter 31

Reece had yet to be given the crystals to put into the breastplate or a weapon he could use in the human likeness and his beast. Reece was shaping the breastplate like a boomerang. He fashioned many pieces in the same shape, stacking and spreading them out to be movable while working as one piece of armor. It would break off if shot but would only break the top level, which would spring off its lever and ricochet to hit the opponent who shot at him. Inside would be the protective multicolored metal to keep his vitals from being harmed.

Quiver dropped the arm plates made with an opening for the sword to dip into when the Overlord transformed into its beast. The lever would allow the Overlord's beast to hold the blade in its mouth if it wanted, or it would snap the sword on the shoulder of his beast for any attacker to meet when they charged at him.

"I think we are making the weapon too effective for him." Quiver sighed. "We aren't supposed to let him win the war."

"I am making it look perfect. Nothing is infallible, especially when you know the Achilles heel of it.

"Ah! You are brilliant."

"No, just careful. I have a lot at stake with this. My

family's lives depend on me following through on my promises. On fixing where I failed them by being led by my lust for adrenaline and girls."

Quiver raised an eyebrow. "I don't think that quality about you has changed."

"Maybe not, but I am trying to put it in the right places."

"I don't know. Are you kissing a Cambion? That's a death sentence for most magicals. I'm told she drains us dry and turns us into shriveled raisins. And if you sleep with them, they are insatiable. Some men have died in pleasure when mating with a Cambion."

"I would be fine. I'm not a normal magical."

"Yeah, that's what we all say until the Cambion-twisted magic is broken. You know her kind is more seductive than a vampire, right? She makes you want her the more time you spend alone with her—makes her irresistible."

"I was hoping it was the opposite." He smirked.

"I thought you said you didn't like her, that what you felt was borderline hate. How does that change?" Quiver tossed another piece of the overlay to the breastplate he'd been working on to Reece. "I'm being observant. You, my friend, are under a spell."

Reece wondered if that were possible. He had every reason to hate Ora. She'd killed his girlfriend and threatened to kill him, and now, he craved her presence every moment. She was still warned that she would destroy him if he showed any signs of causing a virus. He'd wondered what held her back. If he were in her place, he would have killed him in a second.

"I'm not under a spell. I have too many other things to worry about. Love isn't possible for me. I can't go home, and I won't have cursed children. After this is over, I will be destroyed."

Quiver stepped closer and whispered to Reece. "Take that back. Life – human life — is a gift. You have human blood in you; I smell it. As long as it's there and you give your life to the Vigilant, you can live forever, free of this place and the abyss that calls to the rest of us."

"That's what I was promised, but Jeb also told me I will always have to battle my nature; it's not going away. I'm dangerous, more than you know. There is no place for me."

"Well, maybe you and the Cambion are meant to be. Love, they say, conquers all."

Reece snorted. "You've been alone too long. When this is over, you need to find someone, your bonded or something like that."

"I don't know if I'm ready for that. I'd settle for a girlfriend." Quiver elbowed Reece. "I'm next to talk to the Overlord alone."

"Be careful. He probes your mind."

"Then I'm in trouble."

Reece frowned. "Maybe I can help you. I can connect to your thoughts and put up a barrier for you."

"I don't know. If he finds out, he'll know you are different, and everything we've done will be exposed. He'll come after you."

"He doesn't even know my real name. He thinks my

name is Cade."

"Are you strong enough to pull it off? He's taking me in an hour."

"I hope so. Unless you've got any other ideas."

"I've got none. I'll let you in."

"Okay, but before I do it, make me a promise."

"Anything."

"Don't call me master." Reece nailed Quiver's gaze with his. With that widening, Reece pushed his consciousness into Quiver's mind. In there, he built walls filled with his essence, the protection he'd erected within his own.

Chapter 32

They'd planned to meet in Reece's room after they finished working on their weapons. Quiver hadn't been seen since lunchtime, and Ora was trying to get information from the guards on where the Queen's Pendant was hidden. Reece had put more energy into protecting Quiver's secrets than he thought possible. He'd lain on the bed to use as little power as possible to help Quiver through his battle with the Overlord.

Closing his eyes, he placed himself seated within Quiver's mind and could see everything the Overlord did and spoke.

Are you friends with Cade? The boy who can touch the magniton?

"Not really. I like his work, and he lets me help him since I am unworthy to touch the metal. It's, uh…an honor to make them for you, Your Highness."

How did you come here? Were you in the Leopard colony? They have some talent there.

"But they are all gone. Those of us who didn't fall sick with the virus."

Do you know what happened to her - the one who started it? She's been missing a long time.

"No, but I know of the destruction she left behind. Entire tribes we've had to kill to stop the spreading. I thought the Soul Warriors were going to clean up the virus."

They have. As for Zamina, she's been fixed and tested. She had a guard and had been contained. We allowed her to go to school and live her first life amongst other magicals and humans.

"I am glad your warriors are taking care of it. I'd like to finish making the weapons you wanted."

One more thing.

"Yes."

In the lab...there was a fire. We haven't found those who have broken through our defenses – yet. But when we do, they will be given to the abyss.

"You can see magicals to the abyss?" Quiver was getting scared. Reece couldn't speak to him – the Overlord would know.

I can do that or consume the magic that created you. Where would that leave you? Give me a name, a clue to what you see in the weaponsmith. Is it Cade? The human? Or one of the others. Someone stole some of the magniton. That could be the culprit. Was it you?

"No. Why would I do that? If I could make a weapon for you with the magniton, I would be protected. I could return home."

If you want to return home, you will find out who took the magniton and destroyed my lab. Do you understand me?

Yes, My Lord, I understand.

Reece sat up. His head hurt, and he was weaker than he'd ever felt. He needed to feed, but finding the garden entrance was getting more urgent now than ever.

The door opened, and Ora stepped in. "What's wrong with you?"

"The Overlord. I had to protect Quiver's thoughts from him during his interrogation."

"I think I got us a clue to where the queen's pendant is." Ora stood next to where Reece lay on the bed.

Reece fought against closing his eyes.

"You look sick. You're sweating, and your skin is gray."

"It's that bad?" He hated himself, but he didn't have a choice but to ask. "Ora, can you come closer so I can breathe in your magic?"

"You are asking me if you can feed from me?"

He swallowed, realizing she was withholding her magic, pulling it back into herself.

"Yes, you can kill me when this is all over." He pushed himself up on the pillows." But please help me through this. My family needs to go to the Earth Realm, and I can't get them there until this is done and the Overlord is stopped."

"Only if you can do the same for me." Ora crossed her arms.

"What do you mean?"

She sighed. "I mean, we go all the way. I also feed off you. I never did with Zamina, but with you, I feel attracted, like I could without hurting you. You've awakened the hunger of the succubus within me. It's not as strong as my father's desire, but it is there. No other magical would be able to resist or maybe survive through my first feed, but I believe you could."

"What if I don't?"

Ora closed her eyes. "I know how to stop it."

"How?"

"I'd remove the necklace Jeb gave you and deal with the wrath of what you have become without it."

"Okay. Are you sure?"

She studied him for a moment. "I'm sure."

"Before we do this, I need to know something." Reece struggled, but he slid off the bed and stood before Ora. He put his hands on the inner curve of her neck and shoulders, tracing his thumbs along her jaw. "How do you feel about me now? Or, if we weren't where we are now?"

Her lashes fluttered. "I could fall in love with you if I allowed myself. You are the only one I've met who isn't scared of me. I think you are still angry with me about Zamina, and I understand that anger being there. It keeps my heart realistic, reminding me that you could never love me. So, I can give you what you need, and you can give me what I want."

That hurt. It really bothered him. She confirmed she had an attraction and feeling for him but didn't think he could feel them for her. She wanted to use his body to feed her need as an Incubi halfling since she thought he wouldn't die from it.

"That's more than I could hope for, right? You basically want my body." Reece leaned closer to her, inhaling the bit of magic that escaped during her declaration, realizing it confirmed her vulnerability. "But I just want you." He kissed her softly because he wanted to cherish this, their first and last time possibly together like this. Reece vowed that after this, he wanted more for her. He wanted her to fall in love with him.

He felt invincible. Ora lay resting from their power exchange, and he'd survived. It was one of the most intense and addictive moments of his life. As twisted and wrong as it was to fall deeply into this connection with another after being turned by a vampire, he knew, without a doubt, that she would have killed him as a human.

Tears had fallen from her eyes as she told him he'd been made for her. His heart twitched at her words. He pulled her close in his arms and kissed her without taking magic. Looking at her sleeping form filled him with longing to do it all again.

Her eyes opened, and she scrambled away from him to cover her eyes with her hands. "Are my eyes glowing?"

"Yes, but they don't hurt me." Reece grasped her hand and moved it from in front of her eyes. "They're beautiful. You're beautiful."

She tucked the covers up to her neck. "Are you okay? I mean, are you changed?"

"I'm fine. Stronger, not weak like when I battled the Overlord in Quiver's mind. You know, I'm thinking about what you said to me."

Her eyes widened, and she dropped her gaze to her hand that rested in her lap.

"You said I was made for you? Do you feel that way?"

Ora shrugged. "I meant that no other could have withstood my release of magic during the time when we, uh..."

"Made love?"

She frowned at him. "You don't love me."

Reece smiled, noting she didn't admit to not loving him. "I am feeling like I could be falling in love. It's the craziest thing, considering how complicated we are, but I can't help what I feel. I'm fighting against it, but honestly, no one knows me now like you do. I'm still figuring out my new self, learning my abilities, my issues – but you gave me the most special gift you could give – yourself."

"I could have killed you, especially if you were human. I took from you and released my magic without consideration for those around me. I have never done that before."

"But you trusted me enough to do it with me."

"I tested your abilities and couldn't help myself. Trust wasn't my reason. Wanting you was." She turned away from him and started to slide off the bed.

Reece wrapped his arm around her waist and pulled her back. His chin rested on her shoulder, and he kissed her there. "I'm not letting you go. I did this because I am falling in love with you. It's not perfect, and it's messy, but my feelings for you started before this journey. I felt a pull when I first met you, but you pushed that away. Then I focused on the girl who seemed to want me. But in the deep recesses of my heart, my mind, I wanted a chance with you. I knew it wasn't possible."

"What will we have? You should want to avoid being with a Cambion. I can't have children. There is no other magical alive like me to create a child. I will only suck your magic, your strength."

"The beauty is, yes, you do, but I am strong enough to give it and take it back. It's the most intense and giving experience I've ever had. I don't want children. I want you."

He nudged her chin toward his and kissed her. Unchecked tears from her eyes mixed with their kiss, which was the sweetest thing. He tasted her love in those tears she shed while trying to hide it from him.

Reece wouldn't let her feel alone; he'd fall with her. "I love you, Ora."

Chapter 33

A knock sounded on the door. Ora was in the shower, and Reece had just put on his shoes. It was earlier than the call to go to work on the weapons.

Reece opened the door. "Why so early?"

Unoi was there with his arms crossed, tapping his feet. "Quiver is missing."

"What? He was supposed to return to the rooms after meeting with the Overlord."

"I think the Overlord is keeping him."

Exhaling, Reece closed his eyes. "That's not good. The Overlord is trying to find out who blew up the lab and who took the magniton. I can lock in on him to find out where he is. We need to get him out of there."

"If we do, he'll have to be taken somewhere."

"I can do that."

"What can I do to help?"

"Make your weapon, and be prepared to fight with it."

"Got it."

Reece closed the door. Pacing the room, he tried to connect to Quiver. It was hard, like poking into the dark, until he heard a faint whisper. I am in a cage. The room is hot, near boiling, where the castle is warmed. *They want me to transform into my beast. Pain, it's too great.*

Ora came out of the bathroom fully dressed, her hair in a tight knot.

"We have to save Quiver. I know where he is, but I can't go get him without giving our connection away."

"I can get him. You can speak to each of us mentally. You may have to call DewOfWinter to remove him when I find his location."

"Are you sure? It would put you in danger. I don't want that."

"Not your choice, remember? I am doing my job, what I am meant to do. If Quiver becomes compromised, we all are found out."

"Okay, let me show you where he is on the map." Reece went over to the side of the bed and grabbed the cluster of maps from under the bedframe. He placed them on the bed. Sifting through them, he quickly glanced at each. "This one, here." Reece pointed while Ora stood beside him. "This is the entrance to the transfer cells. I think it's where they hold magicals until they move them to dungeons elsewhere. The tunnels go there." Reece called to DewOfWinter. She appeared in an instant with a minuscule amount of mist.

He pointed at the map. "DewOfWinter, can you take Ora here?" Reece smelled the sea-salted aura of her magic as she stood on the other side of him.

"Hmm, yes. There may be turbulence. They seem to have an extra magical barrier around their prisons."

"Take Quiver to the tunnels near here. I think that sculpture leads to the hidden garden that was condemned."

"Will do."

Reece watched Ora and DewOfWinter disappear then left his room to get Unoi.

Unoi was pacing the hall. "I thought you were waiting until it was time to go. I couldn't go back to my room."

"I have someone working on Quiver. He's trapped; they are interrogating him still."

"This isn't good."

"No, but we can't give away that we know or care about it." Reece nodded at Unoi.

"I can try. I am going ahead of you to the workroom. How do you know they aren't spying on us?"

Reece smiled. He'd protected the hall and his room since he'd gotten there. It was natural now that he had done it for so long.

"I've got it covered."

Unoi looked doubtful but hurried out of the hall and through the door. Reece took his time, ensuring he gave them lots of space before opening the door. The usual guard was waiting for him. A Berserker with bottom teeth that curved over his upper lip and under his pointed nose growled. His bushy eyebrows on slanted eyes accentuated his animal-human appearance. Reece just followed him, his mind pinpointed on Quivers. His friend was scared and in pain as the Cyclops guarding him burned his pale skin to get him to transform into his beast. They'd found a hair, something left behind that clued them in that it was a shifter, but they needed Quiver to change. Reece took on some of that pain. It hurt bad, but he forced his expression to remain placid as he walked over to his workstation.

Reece thinned his lips as he went to the fire pit to light his formed sword and split his focus to touch Ora, who was in the tunnels just outside the room. They were holding Quiver. Reece warned her of the number of guards. Quiver counted when he was taken in. DewOfWinter was next to Ora. They were forming a plan for Ora to grab hold of Quiver and DewOfWinter to take them both. Ora reached out to the Mist One, surprised when DewOfWinter changed the plan and went to grab Quiver, leaving Ora behind in the tunnels.

Grunting, Reece lost connection with Quiver and latched on to Ora, telling her to return to the workhouse before she was noticed to be gone. She agreed but was met by a Mole. Reece lost contact with her as she fought it.

Reece slammed down his hammer harder than he intended as he shaped the sword. One of the Gnomes approached him. "Are you alright, lad?"

"Yeah." Reece exhaled. "What do you have for me?"

"The crystals. Everyone has been talking about the superb work you did on the breastplate. The sword, the leg plates, and the shoulder covers are more than the Overlord could have imagined. You are talented. These crystals each have their own energy enhancement abilities that the Overlord can use. Weld them into the armor and weapons for optimum power."

Reece nodded; he was resistant to putting them in. Ora

touched his mind, and he bent his head to close his eyes. *Reece? This is close to the chamber with the queen's pendant. We can come back tonight.*

Then it would happen under cover of night. They would get what they needed and escape. The Overlord may get his armor, but he wouldn't be able to use the enhancements of his crystals. Reece reached in the sack for the crystals the Overlord wanted him to put into his armor and dropped them in his pocket instead.

Chapter 34

Reece pressed his thoughts further, reaching for Quiver's mind.

I'm sorry.

There is nothing to be sorry about. Are you okay?

No. When you left my mind, he pressed in on me. Reece, he knows your real name, and he was pissed.

It could all fall to pieces on them now. Reece's heart pumped faster in his chest. Did the Overlord remember his father? His dad, Max Lewis, was once a Soul Thief from a long line of them but had defected by becoming a Vigilant. If the Overlord knew his real name, then his days were numbered.

Reece paced the room, waiting for Ora to arrive. He saw her briefly earlier, talking to some of the Gnomes, but ignored her presence to keep their relationship hidden.

Ora came in and shut the door. "I know where it is."

"How?"

"Wykwor sent me a message. It is near the Sandman prison. Even though that place unsettles me, we must go back. The entrance to the jewel room can only be reached through there and from the Overlord's wing."

"Unoi is coming."

"Where is Quiver?"

"DewOfWinter put him someplace safe within the tunnels. I have his location; he refused to leave without us. Quiver told me he'd come to us when he recovered. DewOfWinter is looking for the entrance to the garden. I gave her one of the maps."

The knock on the door was rapid. Ora opened it, and Unoi came in. "I think we will have to run sooner than we thought."

"Why?"

"The guards are searching for Quiver." He cleared his throat. "Thanks to a message I sent to Megan, she sent dragons to start a distraction, and now they're attacking the outer gates. It would have been safer for us if the Overlord wasn't holding Quiver so long."

"We can get him, but we can't leave without the queen's pendant. Get everything you need; we may not be coming back."

Ora grabbed her weapon's belt, and Unoi shrugged. "I got all I need on me now. I'm always ready."

Reece moved the dresser in front of the door and then the chair. Unoi pushed the bed forward. Ora took off her glasses and welded the door shut.

"This is it. Let's go." Reece led the way to the tunnels. Unoi closed the door and followed. With Ora's full essence consumption, Reece's abilities were even more enhanced. He could smell what was in the tunnel more vividly than before. His senses were heightened.

208

They traveled quickly to the room with the Sandmen. This time, when they tried to move the door that allowed them entrance to the closet, it was sealed closed. Reece pointed at the door. Unoi climbed over him to get to it. Unoi placed a hand on the door, and it dissolved. Reece followed him into the closet of the room. He heard the beeping. The movement was faint under the distraction of the beep and tapping of feet. At least four guards were in there. Reece put up four fingers. The others nodded. Everyone knew there was no going back.

Unoi got out first. Reece held up his hand for Ora to wait until Unoi gave them the signal. A magical with green hair, tusks protruding from his mouth, and clawed feet and hands growled at Unoi. Its pointed ears flicked its wild hair as it bent to charge Unoi. The magical met the blade of Unoi's magniton knife. The slice down its face made it angry. It wound its club from behind to swing at Unoi. Like a reptile, a female with a green-scaled face snatched her whip at Unoi. Reece jumped out of the closet to catch it. His speed surprised her, but she recovered to hit him with another whip with her other hand. Reece took the blow. The cut his arm didn't stop his pull on the rope to snatch her forward. They butted heads, and she raked her nails down his face. Reece roared, kneed her, then kicked her into one of the cases.

Someone stabbed him in the shoulder from behind. Reece pivoted with a kick. The grey guard with a metal mask growled, flicking its long tail covered in magniton. The guard whipped its tail, and Reece grabbed the middle and yanked. It twitched, and hooks sprung from the tip. The guard reared back a few feet then leaped onto Reece. Reece let go of the tail and snatched his dagger from his pocket to throw it at the neck of the guard.

"Yah!" It sliced him in the neck, but the guard snatched it out, tossed it to the ground, and charged Reece with his teeth bared.

Someone grabbed Reece from behind the woman. Her sharp nails nicked his throat. His necklace revealed itself.

"What do we have here?" She flicked it.

"Don't touch that!" Reece reared back, smacking his head into her chin. He kicked one leg up, hitting the male guard in the chest. Reece braced himself against the guard as he sliced down into his thigh. He lost control. Blood pulsed through his veins. Power gushed through him, and he was hungry. His teeth sliced through his gums, his mouth opened twice its size, and the magical who cut his leg hesitated. With lightning speed, Reece surged forward and latched onto his arm. Strong, dark magic filled his nostrils, thick blood with the taste of ash filled his mouth, and it was filling. With each draw, the hits, cuts, and stabs from the female met rock. He'd healed, and his skin had hardened to create an almost impregnable armor.

The guard was drained dry, and Reece had grown several inches in height and thickness. He turned to the female and smiled. "You wanted to see my necklace?" Reece's hands were thick with black nails, sharpened at the end. "Come and get it." He grabbed her by the arm. She tried to raise her spear to stab him again. He was full but inhaled her magic, and its minty taste made him smack his lips. She'd weakened, turning limp. Reece took another drag in of her then stabbed her in the arm with her spear.

Reece turned around and stopped at Ora's stricken expression. There was fear in her eyes as she looked up at him. Unoi was still fighting off someone in the distance.

"Your face, eyes, teeth…you look so different."

"I do." He inhaled slowly to calm his rage and willed himself back to his human form. Reece felt a retreat within his body, the power it collected compressed and settled deeply into a ball.

Unoi came alongside him. "That was the last of them."

"Good. Can you unlock any of these cases?" Reece walked over to the red-haired male, who looked like Megan. "Him, is there a way to weaken this case? The magic keeping him here?"

"There is a legend that only one Rumpelstiltskin can live at one time. But Megan is Rumpelstiltskin and Fae, she might not qualify as a full Rumpelstiltskin. If we release her father, he may be able to convince her to back down." Ora tapped her feet.

"I'll try, but we don't have time to sit around to see if it works."

Reece stood behind Unoi as he watched his purple hand glow and his magic press forward to the case's flat base that had a magical inscription etched in it.

"That should do it."

"Fine. I'll call DewOfWinter to clean this up." Reece reached for DewOfWinter, and she came, but this time with friends. Two females dressed like Genies: one with long dark hair and brown skin, the other with almond-toned skin, slanted eyes, and thick green hair.

"My sisters, they are helping me learn the castle. We found the entrance to the garden." DewOfWinter smiled.

Reece bent and picked up his dagger from the floor. He wiped the blood off it and onto his black pants. "Thanks. We will need you to take us there after we get the queen's pendant."

The Mist Ones glanced at each other. DewOfWinter laughed. "You will need more of us to clean up the mess of guards you'll face protecting that."

Her sisters giggled. Then one bared her teeth's jagged points. "I guess we'll eat well tonight." She opened her mouth. Her body turned to mist. Her head and teeth remained, biting the head off the fallen guard as mist wrapped around the body and disappeared.

"Your sister is different than you?" Reece blinked then looked up at DewOfWinter.

"No, she just likes her hair green." DewOfWinter smiled. "And she likes to scare others."

Reece shook his head at her dry humor and waved to the others to follow him. The room with the tombs of sandmen had a connecting door to a hallway with paintings of past queens. The pictures were of females who had a human look yet a glow through their hair, pointed ears, or alluring beauty. The current Overlord's deceased wife was beautiful. Although she was human, she held a regal air of strength that settled around her, making her seem more magical than the others.

"She is the veil or barrier that keeps magicals from breaching the earthen realm."

"Her jewels would be in here?" Reece pushed the door. He'd pressed against it. The door felt like leather. It had no doorknob. It was warm to the touch.

DewOfWinter popped in next to him. "I could help you get in, get the pendant, and to the garden."

"Yes, you could."

"But it will come at a price. Can you pay for it? Give the Mist Ones a part in your war against the Overlord?"

"I can pay that."

"Yes, but there is one more thing we need."

"What?"

"Don't give her anything." Unoi raised a hand. "The Mist Ones are fickle allies."

DewOfWinter stepped in front of Unoi. "The crystals. We need them as a bargaining tool to free those imprisoned by the Overlord."

"Deal. When we get to the garden – alive." Reece laughed.

DewOfWinter put a hand on his arm. "You don't realize it, do you?"

"What?"

"You are more powerful than you know. I couldn't consume you if I wanted to. There is something in you. Deep within, it shines and destroys magic that tries to touch it. You are holding it back, and when it releases – you could destroy the Overlord, even the Rumpelstiltskin – the two most powerful beings in The Void."

Reece shook his head and moved back. "I don't know what I am capable of. I'm still discovering the new me, and there is much I don't like."

"I see." She stepped back. "Who's first?"

"Me." Reece held Ora's hand. "Then her and Unoi."

She nodded and turned into a thick mist. Reece knew having the Mist One's alliance was invaluable. The closer he got to completing his purpose, the more his heart clenched at the thought of having to leave Ora behind. If DewOfWinter was right, Ora might not be able to sustain the full brunt of his unique essence.

Chapter 35

DewOfWinter dropped him from the ceiling of the Crown Jewels room. He landed quietly in the far corner. She slid in behind the guards standing in front of the jewelry cases in the center of the room. One of the guards turned at the light noise. Reece threw his dagger at the magical with the scaled face of a snake. It pierced one of its eyes.

The creature made a gurgling sound that alerted the other two creatures. They had the bodies of men with the necks and faces of cobras. Their heads and tongues struck out before their bodies moved. Reece blocked a tongue with his arm, and the sting of it felt like a knife. Unoi jumped out behind him and created a whip of light with his magic that cut off the tongues of two of the creatures.

Unoi turned his magic ropes into glowing swords in each of his hands. It sliced through the necks of two oncoming snake heads. Ora flipped over Unoi's attack to kick one and then the other in the stomach.

Reece called DewOfWinter. She and her sisters popped in, grabbed the other three approaching snake men, and disappeared with them. Only the six dead ones remained on the floor.

"That's over, but the jewels have magic locks on them." Ora stood in front of the queen's crown suspended in the air. The scepter and pendant necklace were suspended in other areas of the room. Underneath each were sharp pieces of glass protruding from the ground.

"Any idea how to get this out?" Reece scratched his head.

"I think I know how." Unoi scratched at the bandage that covered his chin. "It will take a sacrifice of magic."

"What about the crystals? I can use one of them. They enhance ability."

"Unless they stop that glass from the blood sea, it can't help."

"How do you know it's from the blood sea?" Reece tilted his head to study the pieces.

"The color. The glass is mirrored, and if you look closely, there is a mirror within a mirror. The inner image from the mirror within the glass is so horrible that it will reflect around this room, turning all of us to stone."

"I think I can help." Ora stepped up between them. "I can reflect images or magic away from me."

"Okay, but Unoi said this would reflect around the room."

"There is one thing we can do, but it would be unpleasant." Unoi walked around one of the dead reptile men. "The scales on their skin reflect light and magic, which is why they were the species here to protect the jewels."

"We don't have time to pick off scales." Reece glanced

down at the fallen guard.

"No, but if we surround ourselves with the bodies and Ora uses her power to reflect, we should be good. My magic will hold them up to stand around us, and Ora can do the rest."

"Then do it." Reece dragged one of the bodies up to a sitting position. Unoi's magic wrapped each of the four dead reptile creatures and lifted them straight to standing with eyes open. He arranged them around them, and they squeezed inside. Reece was close enough to the pendant to reach his hand between the reptile shield of bodies to grasp it.

"How do we know an alarm won't go off through the castle?"

Unoi shrugged. "It will, so be quick to grab the pendant."

"Alright." Reece hoped the plan worked. "Ora, your stick." He reached for her guard stick that extended when the button was pushed to a spear. "Ready?"

"As ever," Unoi replied, and the bodies of reptile creatures locked in place.

"Yes, my reflective shield is up." Ora touched Reece with her elbow.

Reece tapped the pendant. The rod had turned to stone. It swayed, and the glass on the floor unlocked from its places and sprang up, levitating, beams shot out from them, reflecting on the walls, and the room was encased in rock.

"They are still activated." Reece cursed. "I'm going to get it."

"You'll turn to stone," Ora warned.

"Only my hand." Reece reached out quickly and snatched the pendant. An intensely cold pain coated his skin. He called for DewOfWinter.

She came in a flash. Her fog wrapped around him, and she screamed. "Your skin burns like arctic ice!"

"Bare it! Take me now!" DewOfWinter groaned. Reece lost the sensation of his body as he felt it separate and reform itself from the transport within DewOfWinter. She dropped him on the floor and fell to her knees next to him.

"You were poisoned!"

"A trap." Reece lifted his hand, the pendant was there, but his hand was gray. "Will it spread?"

"It can. You must feed to heal."

"How do you know?"

"When I transport someone, I instinctively know their cells I pull apart so they can be put back together again. You must feed now."

Two grey clouds appeared. DewOfWinter's sisters dropped Ora and Unoi on the floor. They stepped aside in unison and bowed to DewOfWinter.

"The alarms were sounded. They've released the Gargoyles."

"We have to go." DewOfWinter waved at her sisters. "Gargoyles are the only magicals besides the Overlord who can see, track, and kill us."

Reece nodded.

Ora rushed over to him. "Reece! It's spreading!"

Reece watched his skin turn grey. It felt numb, and he could barely move.

Tears fell from her eyes. "No...no, I can't lose you like this."

"You—can I feed from you? It has to be different this time. I need the blood and the magic to heal myself."

"Yes, yes!" Ora ripped at the collar on her shirt and bent down for him to grasp her with his other hand.

He drank, and – God help him – she was the most delicious meal he'd tasted. When they'd mated, he only took the magic she spilled upon him, but this was way beyond what they'd done before. He felt invincible and honestly couldn't drink more of her. The blood, the magic, sat so heavy within him that he almost wanted to sleep. He retracted his teeth and fell back onto the ground. Reece's hand tingled with heat.

"He's healing instantly." Unoi gasped.

Ora bent over him and kissed him. "I...I love you." Tears dripped from her eyes.

"And I, you." He exhaled and pushed himself up. The statue in front of them was of the former queen, which explained why the Overlord never went into this castle wing. It must have been hers. Reece placed the pendant into his pocket.

In a puff of mist, Quiver was dropped in front of the statue, his face haggard, but he was well.

"You're alright?" Reece was glad to see him. He hugged

him and patted his shoulder.

"Nearly dying, and you finally act like I'm your friend," Quiver chuckled. "Let's get into the garden."

"We are trying; it's not working."

They all touched parts of the statue they could reach. Quiver stood back from them, and Reece turned. "Are you helping?"

"How tall was she?"

"Maybe around six-foot-five. Only a small bit shorter than the Overlord." Ora tapped the statue's feet.

"Then the lever would be within her reach." Reece touched the jeweled belly button on the statue of the former queen before pressing in. The figure sank into the wall and then slid to the side to reveal a lush garden entrance lined with trees on both sides. A creaking sound came from behind them as the statue closed the door and returned to its place to reveal another statue of the former queen in a regal stance and head tilted to the side.

Chapter 36

The garden was a vast maze. On each side of the entrance were large coned-shaped trees. A gate was unlocked. Reece walked up to it. He smelled the air then touched the handle, knowing that Zamina had been the last one there.

"This way." Reece pushed the gate open. The others followed in silence. The place seemed huge, but from the garden map and what he remembered being told, it was an illusion. It was as if the person who designed the garden had it used it as a cover for an escape. Zamina had stumbled upon the exit to the forest by accident.

"I hate mazes." Unoi snorted.

"I've never been in one." Ora turned around then came to face Reece. "She kept this a secret for six months or more."

"Probably longer. She told me she was held in her rooms for a while before she was allowed to go school but was able to have some freedom roaming the maze." Reece noted the red-hued sky and the smell of something odd in the air.

They continued to walk down the center of the aisle, which was lined by thick, high bushes along with statues of various animals like wolves, jaguars, cheetahs, bears, and horses. At the end of the path...unicorns. There stood a statue of a man with a beard and arms crossed on his chest. Each of his fingers pointed in opposite directions. Reece knew from the map that each path led to a hidden stairwell from the garden to the woods, but they had different ways of access.

"The right. I think that would be easier." Reece led them down the path. The path grew smaller and tighter. They had to go one by one to squeeze through. Vines were shaped into hands and leaves as nails, grabbed at them. Reece pushed Ora out of the way. They continued to move swiftly from side to side to avoid being touched by the branches.

A vine hand grabbed at Quiver's shoulder.

"Watch out!" Reece called.

Reece and Unoi turned to yank him away from its grip.

The hands shot out, grabbing and ripping their clothes with thorned tips.

"Stay in the middle and walk in a straight line. There is a small area the hands can't reach. It tries harder to grab us if we go off the path." Ora walked on a tightrope. "It's why I haven't been attacked."

Quiver led the way now, calmed after they saved him from one of the hands. Reece let Ora in front of him. Unoi was in the rear. They got to the next bend in the path where they had to decide which direction to go. In the intersection was a wall intertwined with leaves, vines, and blooms shaped in the form of a Centaur female with a body of pale peach blooms and the white shape of a horse. Her hair was yellow roses and her eyes blue.

"Beautiful. I've never seen a female Centaur. The males keep them very protected since there are so few of them." Unoi stepped closer to observe the artful display.

"Her arrow is pointing to the right. Should we go right?" Quiver pointed.

"No. The map directed us to go the opposite way," Reece said.

Ora turned and started down the path. Reece followed. The thick bushes held a mixture of flowers that looked like groupings, including alocasia, coleus, impatiens, and cuphea. Reece narrowed his eyes at the flowers because they had a magic hue around them. They weren't normal. Before he could warn Ora, one of the blooms opened its mouth, and teeth protruded. Another opened and spat out a spore that landed in Ora's neck.

"Ouch!" She smacked at her shoulder where the spore landed. "What was that?"

"The flower, it spits it at you." Quiver partially shifted into his beast, baring his teeth and claws. "It's poison! Are you okay?" Quiver growled at the retreating flower. "You have to reveal your magic, and it will leave you alone. We have these irritating blooms in our forest."

Reece let his incisors drop. Ora took off her glasses and snatched the spore out of her neck. Unoi's eyes glowed.

"I don't feel." Ora tripped on the grass.

"Ora, change." Reece reached for her.

"I can't." her voice sounded winded.

The flowers hissed at them as they passed but didn't spit

any more spores. Reece placed a hand on Ora's shoulder. She was stumbling and fell. He surged forward to catch her before she could collapse.

"What happened?" Quiver rushed up to walk alongside Reece.

"A spore got her in the neck." Reece got to the end of the corridor as fast as possible. It seemed that when they reached a crossroads in the garden, they wouldn't have to worry about traps. He laid her on the ground in front of the enormous tree shaped like a woman. It had lines in the bark like a form-fitting brown gown trimmed in green moss. The branches and tightly grouped burnt orange leaves cascaded around the face of the tree woman like an afro.

Reece laid Ora on the soft grass at the base of the tree woman.

"She's turning blue." Reece felt his eyes water; he couldn't lose her now. "I don't know what to do."

"The poison kills if we don't get it treated. You can save her, though. You're a vampire. You can give her some of your blood." Quiver pointed at Ora.

"If he does that, he will bond to the Cambion. Her magic will wrap around him like a noose and trap him to her even if he resists. No magical can resist the call of a Cambion." He lifted his eyebrow. "That is why they are destroyed."

"I don't care." Reece bit into his wrist and let his blood drip onto her lips. She was deliriously fighting him, refusing his blood. He forced her mouth open and held her while several drops fell in.

"No…you don't know what…you've done." Ora tried to

spit out his blood, but he dropped more in. Finally, she swallowed, gulping it down.

Her eyes glowed, and her color returned, but then she convulsed. His hand glowed white. The glow touched Ora where his hand rested. It skipped over her skin as if testing her, deciding if it wanted to sink into her. Then the glow flattened and seeped into her skin. He could see it traveling through her veins. Suddenly, it burst from her chest in two ribbons of light. It wrapped around Reece and pulled them close together, heart to heart.

Reece hadn't thought his heart had a beat since he'd turned. It had slowed to near death rate, but now it beat faster, taking on the same rhythm as Ora's.

"Oh no, they are bonding! How...did you and Ora mate?" Quiver asked.

"None of your business—"Reece felt a jolt of electricity in his heart. It beat faster, in perfect time with Ora's.

"You did! It's done. They're bonded forever."

Reece stared at Ora's beautiful eyes. The glow that would cause others pain to look at dulled as he and she gazed at each other.

Forever.

Reece, I'm sorry. I should have told you. I tried.

I don't care.

I'm sorry.

There is no one else for me but you.

It's unbreakable.

I'm unbreakable with you - we could be unbreakable.

But I didn't want this for you.

I want it for me.

You don't know what this means.

It means I will love you forever.

But what about…

It's our story. Our story isn't perfect. But my choice to love you in spite of it – is.

Please forgive me. I love you too.

Reece kissed her. Closing his eyes, he whispered, "It's okay."

Chapter 37

Reece made Ora stay behind him. She'd fully recovered, but he wouldn't risk her life again. After he'd given her his blood, he felt connected to her in a much deeper way. She could read him intuitively. He felt safer with her behind him. She'd moved behind him and nodded as though she'd heard his thoughts before he made the effort to share them.

They'd taken the path lined with trees. These trees were unlike any Reece had seen. They were all in the likeness of humans, with moss, flowers, and leaves of different colors to adorn them in ways that made them appear clothed. All had indentations in their bark resembling eyes, but they were closed.

"Are they sleeping?" Unoi turned in a circle as he studied them.

"Yeah. I feel their magic, but it is dormant. It is seeping from the roots they share between them. I think they are communicating that way." Reece sniffed the air. "They are aware of us, though."

"One of them peeked at me." Quiver elbowed Unoi.

"Just keep walking. We are halfway through."

"I hope so." Unoi snorted. "Can't you call the Mist Ones

to help us?"

"No, they have to know where they are going. None of them know the way out of here, and they can't pop in or out. A barrier of magic keeps the creatures in here from escaping." Reece pointed to the sky. "Can you see that film of pink?"

Yes, now I can, through your eyes.

"I can't." Unoi looked up.

"Me neither." Quiver put his hand up to shield his eyes.

They heard whispering between the trees. As fast as Reece could turn from one to another of the trees, the lips etched within their barks shut tight. All at once, the leaves rustled, and the ground shook.

"They are waking." Reece placed a hand up for them to stop moving. "Be still. See what they are going to do."

"Eat us, crush us, or maybe they want to fill the air with poison. Let's run." Quiver shrugged and snorted.

"No, we have to remain calm to get out of here. Every passage has clues."

"Just great. I survive torture to become a sitting duck for tree people." Quiver pivoted.

"Let them wake first." Reece waited. Finally, one of the trees'—dressed as a male with brown and green leaves—eyes opened. The eyes were the color of his leaves, brown intertwined with green.

"Can you tell me if another passed this way?" Reece asked, hoping he didn't seem intimidating.

"Not in a while." The tree's voice sounded ancient.

"Is there a way out of here to take us to a cabin?"

The tree-male closed his eyes.

"They don't want to help. C'mon." Reece led the way forward. Their feet didn't make a sound on the thick grass. Reece frowned, noticing that the roots of the trees were starting to protrude from the grass.

"They are moving." Ora pointed.

"More like closing in on us." Unoi flicked his hand, and flames danced from it. "I will set them on fire."

"Don't." Reece raised his hand. "It's important that we aren't attacked by them. This is the way out."

Behind them, the trees were sliding through the grass, vines lifted from the thick sod. The trees closed them off from being able to retrace their steps. In front of them, a root popped from the ground. One of the trees rose to reveal trunks shaped like legs and feet. It yanked its trunk from the ground, spraying dirt upward.

"Can I burn them now?" Unoi asked.

"No, just run. Don't let it block us from getting to the end." Reece grabbed Ora's hand and pulled her. They dodged through the trees trying to block their way. Hands shaped from tree limbs tore at their skin, blocking their path. Reece grabbed Ora by the waist and leaped onto the branch of the nearest tree. Adjusting his hold on her, he jumped from limb to limb.

"How are you doing that?"

"I don't know." Reece jumped down. Another tree's limb

whipped out and snatched Ora from his grasp.

Ora wrestled from it, then kicked it and flipped away.

It was shaped like a female with her head down. A cascade of green and yellow leaves flowed from its shoulder. They moved in unison as she mimicked him to land on the grass in front of the last tree.

"Ow!" Quiver fell to the ground behind them.

Unoi slid through two tree limbs and flipped to stand next to Reece.

"Glad you made it, guys."

The tree at the dead end lifted its head. Its eyes remained closed. "You want passage?"

"Yes. The map showed a secret passage to a cabin in the woods." Reece stood in front of the tree.

"There are many ways to where you seek to go. Why did you come to me?"

"My friend traveled this path. She told me to come to the cabin by the tree path." Reece reached into his pocket and took out a small crystal. "She told me to present a gift. This is all I have."

"What are you doing? Don't give her your crystals."

"I am giving her one as a gift. The others are meant for the Mist Ones." Reece lifted his palm to her extended branch arm.

Reece dropped the emerald-shaped jewel into her hand.

"How did you know which one I would have wanted?"

"It's the color of your magic."

"You have made a wise choice. Therefore, you may ask me three questions."

"Can you tell me if there are other ways to enter the castle through the garden?"

"Yes, this garden has several entrances and exits. The tree path is one, the dead-sea path is another, and the Gargoyle path is the last."

"Is there a way to bypass the danger of each path?"

The tree smiled. "You are indeed a smart one. Yes, you must present your gift before you start down the path to the gatekeeper."

"Can you open the gate for us now?"

"Yes." The middle of her trunk opened to reveal a stairwell. Reece took the first step. Ora and the others followed.

Inside the tree, the stairwell was golden and smelled of freshly cut wood. There was no railing, but it wound down in a circular direction. He could see the bottom ended at the top of a cloud. Reece jumped off the step and into the clouds. The freefalling experience was short as he landed on moss-covered rock—a rock formation of stairs. Taking each step through the cool mist, he glanced back to make sure Ora was close behind.

His mouth dropped as he noticed many of the Vigilant warriors at the base of the stairs, waiting, cheering as he jumped off the final step. He put out a hand to help Ora down the last step.

"Where's Jeb?" Reece searched the warriors in black form-fitting outfits that reminded him of ninja warriors.

"Here! Here I am." The sea of warriors parted. "What you have done for us is a miracle. We have much to do. Megan's army is taking action. They are storming the sea gate. We must beat them there before the Overlord's magic clashes with hers. It could destroy The Void and cause a tsunami wave that will impact the Earth Realm."

Reece noticed Unoi was slowly moving away and that he had the same bracelet on his wrist that was put on him. With lightning speed, he grasped Unoi's wrist. "Did you send a message to Megan about the castle's location?"

Unoi smiled. "Of course. I finished the job you were sent to do." He lifted the bracelet to his lips to bite down on the beads. "Now she will be dispersing others here, to stop you from interfering."

Reece jerked his arm away from him. Unoi snatched his blade from his belt and stabbed it into Reece's arm. Ora jumped onto his back. Reece elbowed up and twisted out of the range of the burst of magic from Unoi's hand.

He heard a battle roar and turned to see two giant Saber Tigers leap over the crowd of warriors. The enormous black saber tooth tiger with glowing white eyes bit into Unoi's neck, knocking Reece out of the way as it put its foot on Unoi's chest.

The golden saber stood in front of the other. They transformed differently than other shifters he'd seen. Their animal persona fell away from them in a shimmer of light to reveal two angels. One with beautiful dark skin and adorned in a gold warrior dress with white wings and gold rings around her black locks. The other was pale with battle armor and white wings. Reece's jaw dropped at what the angel's wings uncovered.

"Rei?" Tears fell from his eyes as he ran and picked up his sister. He swung her around in a circle as he laughed and cried. "I'm so sorry I almost killed you. Do you forgive me?"

She laughed. "Yes, you goof! I have already forgiven you. You helped me by draining some of the angel's magic. It helped me conceal the power until I really needed it." She hugged him back.

"Bro? When are you going to put her down?" Reece shook his head. It couldn't be. He set Rei down and turned around. His brother Dexter was standing next to Jeb.

"Dex? That you?" He ran to his brother and hugged him.

"In the flesh. Guess who else is here to bring the Overlord's plans to burn?"

"Who?" Reece looked through the crowd of warriors and then put his fist to his mouth to hold back the shame.

His father walked through the crowd. Max Lewis, the only person he'd wanted to grow up to be like. "Dad?" His voice broke. "I'm sorry I did this to our family."

"What are you talking about?"

"I turned into something—someone—who could have killed all of you because I didn't listen to the warnings. I worked for Megan, basically sold my soul to her because I was arrogant and reckless."

"Well, son, you are no different than your siblings or me. We all fell for Megan's lies and coercions. I was recruited by the head scientist for the Overlord and Megan. I thought I handled it, but it's my fault all of you were at risk. They got to me by seeking to recruit you all. My Vigilant brothers saved me and all of us one time too many to have this day of victory."

"Thanks, Dad. Thanks for telling me." He hugged his father, who hugged him back. Then pulled away. "Where's mom and EmVee?" Reece searched the crowd.

"Working in a somewhat 'hostage' situation with Megan to ensure we all end this as peacefully as possible."

"I have the pendant." Reece reached into his pocket and grasped the neckwear. "It's a way to bond the Overlord and Megan. Since they both are at odds, the magic will always be balanced."

Jeb came forward. "That works well with our plan. We also have one other piece that must be completed."

Rei raised her hand. "This is Eli. He holds the *Book of Magic Transfer* that could wrestle Megan's power from her. The Overlord's power too, but only if he is weakened."

"There is a problem with weakening him."

Reece grabbed Ora's hand. "What's the problem?"

"If he is weakened too much, every realm will feel the effects in the erosion of their worlds." Ora squeezed Reece's hand.

"We had to join forces with an ancient magical who can wield the magic in the book of magical transfer." Jeb frowned. "It's not how we Vigilant usually work, but this is not our world. It's only a world we were sent to keep from contaminating our Earth Realm. So, in this, we are forced to let the powers here work within their boundaries."

A black unicorn came forward. It had white hair and a gold horn. It pranced regally down the open path the warriors created. It stood in front of Reece and bowed then transformed into a dark-skinned woman in a gold gown with a diamond trimmed in gold in the middle of her forehead. Her long white hair lay in waves over her shoulders and back.

"Thank you for giving us a way into the Overlord's lair. The war he hopes to incite will destroy us all. There was an agreement that if our forefathers paid for their deeds, we magicals could live peacefully here in The Void. Provided we adhere to certain rules of our nature. There is some bending of those rules here and there, but war is strictly prohibited, or we will all be destroyed by a fate worse than our ancestors."

"We don't have much time. The Overlord knows we left and knows my real name. He may have guards in the garden now. We found Megan's father. He's been turned into a Sandman. Unoi over there—" Reece glanced at Unoi, who was in cuffs and chains— "weakened the locks on his prison, but we aren't sure it will work. Megan believes the Overlord killed her father and is against the war."

The regal unicorn shifter turned to Jeb. "You may call me Perseeha. I need to get to the throne room. Megan and the Overlord should be brought to me there."

"The journey won't be safe. We must go through the gardens."

Reece told Jeb the passkeys to get through the maze. "I also have someone who can help." Reece called to DewOfWinter, and what appeared like fog rolling in covered the sky above them as hundreds of Mist Ones dropped from it.

DewOfWinter dropped in front of Reece. "We are ready. There is a war ensuing now between Megan's forces and the Overlord's on the seaside of the castle where our kin, the Kelpies, were imprisoned."

"You convinced the Mist Ones to help you?" His father raised his eyebrow.

"I've changed." Reece nodded at DewOfWinter. "Have your people take us to the battle."

Chapter 38

It was a fight to the death. Giants, Cyborgs, Gargoyles, Berserkers, and various magicals battled against Megan's warriors, including beast shifters, Fae who stood over seven feet tall, and Faeries who were only several inches tall. Megan's warriors were losing ground. The flat rock path was several yards wide. Thick rocks jutted from the ground on both sides. The trail ended at a bridge that led to the front entrance of the Overlord's castle. Its doors were open, shining a bright orange light like a fire. More Giants and Berserkers were dispersed from the Overlord's magic portal from that firelight.

Reece was delivered in front of Megan's warriors. He would fight alongside her to push back the Overlord's forces. Ora was next to him, battling with a Cyborg. He was shocked at her speed as she ripped off her glasses and hypnotized the creature who was twice her size, ripping through its chest with her sword. Reece felt the sting of a claw in his shoulder and allowed his body to transform. In an instant, his claws were drawn. He jumped, kicking the Berserker in front of him. A burn sparked on his shoulder. He jerked his shoulder from the claws of the Gargoyle who hovered above him. The Overlord's warriors were pressing fast. A dark mist formed above the battlegrounds, and

Vigilant warriors dropped to the flat rock surface in the throes of the battle.

He yanked the Gargoyle by the leg as it tried to dive in and snatch up one of the fairies, slamming it to the ground. His sister Rei dropped from the mist and transformed into a giant Saber Tooth tiger. He didn't feel the transformation, but he was taller and thicker than before. His long hair fell around his shoulders; his skin was taut with a gray tinge. The claws on his fingers itched as he ripped them through one Berserker and dug them into another to balance himself for a kick at the chin of a Cyclops. A shriek louder than the thunder of the battle came from above as Megan rode atop a green and blue Dragon. Her red hair was a wavy mass that flowed behind her as she raised her sword above. The dragon spewed fire on the Overlord's warriors, and they fell back toward the castle's entrance.

Reece fought to get through the remaining push of the Overlord's fighters, which wouldn't relent in their push forward. The Overlord's fighters were viciously grabbing the Fae and biting into them. The Mist Ones dropped from above to envelop the Overlord's beast, saving a Vigilant fighter from a deadly fate.

A Gargoyle lifted Reece by the shoulder. Reece sliced his claws just above the ankle. With a shriek, the creature released him. Another Berserker swung its club at Reece. Reece dropped low, slicing through its stomach, causing it to fall to its knees. Reece slashed it in the throat. He pivoted away and threw his knife into a charging Cyclops' eye. Reece's torso was cut, and his shoulder was sliced to the bone, but Reece was healing faster than before. He felt no pain, just pure energy as he leaped over fighting warriors.

He made it to the entrance when the Overlord in beast form burst through the castle door. His bone mask covered the mouth, but crowded pointed teeth protruded. The armor Reece had made was plated in moveable protective links that covered his chest. When the Overlord's beast rose on its hind legs, the protected shield revealed the multi-colored metal beneath. The crystals were missing from the design that would have provided an extended barrier of magic throughout the armor.

Willing the ruby necklace that held his change at bay, Reece felt it reveal itself on his chest. He ripped at it, but it wouldn't come off. He called to Ora, sensing her presence near as she fought alongside him as a shadow warrior, feeling each of his unconscious thoughts as his bonded mate.

"You need me?" Ora called.

He moved when Ora's back pressed against his. He threw his dagger into the eye of a Gargoyle swooping over them in the attack.

"Rip the necklace off me. It won't let me do it. Must be done by another Vigilant."

Ora pivoted, stood in front of him, and gave him a quick kiss before tearing off the necklace. A Berserker roared behind him and Ora, throwing her sword into the neck of an attacking berserker.

Reece's neck was on fire. Pins of heat barreled through his veins. Not from the vampire but the angelic warrior whose light he'd stolen from his sister during his first feeding. Light illuminated his arms, neck, body.

The Overlord's beast had sprouted wings, and its sword

had lifted to its mouth as it slashed at the dragon Megan rode. They were in a fierce battle, but Megan was losing. Her dragon was bleeding and spitting fire in wild directions, engulfing both sides in flames.

Reece fell to his knees, his arms and fingers aflame with light. His body turned completely white with a glow that should have destroyed his vampiric infection. Those natures warred within him, and he rolled on the ground encased in light while surrounded by those in battle. So many images flooded his brain. He saw everything, but he closed his eyes, fighting to push the images of the battle away.

The force of light around him couldn't be penetrated. Warriors tried to cut through it but were attacked by the Vigilant. Reece's fangs remained. His claws were black but with tips of white. His back was ripped on each side, and under his shoulders, black wings sprouted.

Reece burst through the light and into the sky, his wings working on instinct. He flew higher, catching Megan when her dragon fell from the sky. Reece grabbed the Overlord's slashing sword. A surge of light burst from his hand. He broke the Overlord's sword and flung the pieces back at the beast. The Overlord surged at him. Its jaws extended and bit Reece's arm but couldn't penetrate the flesh.

Reece narrowed his eyes and flexed, feeling a burning lava fill his veins. The Overlord's beast yelped in pain and released him. Reece grabbed the beast by the neck. Squeezing, he reached for the tail then sliced it into its armor, throwing it to the ground. Reece spun the Overlord around by the tail and threw him against the top of the castle, leaving a dent and broken pieces that slid down the front as the Overlord's beast fell to the ground.

Reece dropped from the sky to where the Overlord had fallen. The ground began to shake, and the sky turned red.

"The Overlord's injuries! They are causing him to lose grip on the power to fuel The Void!" Reece, his height now nearly ten feet, picked up the Overlord, whose beast was so giant its feet dragged as he slammed the Overlord's body against the castle wall. Reece ripped the armor from the beast and penetrated the Overlord's mind where an enraged struggle for consciousness took place.

I can trap you here, alive enough to fuel The Void but too weak to live fully. Reece burst through the doors of the castle. The Overlord's warriors moved out of the way as Reece dragged the Overlord in the beast form to the throne room where Jeb and the Unicorn shifter waited.

I will avenge this by killing everyone in your entire lineage, Reece Lewis. I'll start with your father, Max, once my prized Soul warrior. Reece ignored the Overlord's threats. He dropped the Overlord's stiff beast at the foot of Jeb.

The unicorn Oracle's eyes widened at Reece. "You are the prophesized tool of vengeance and protection. Wings of our salvation and the taint of our ancestors. You are the justice the magicals and vigilant have been waiting for – it is you."

"I'm none of those things. I am a mistake caused by the impulsive selfish ways that led me to nearly kill my entire family. I will stay here and do whatever you need me to because I found someone, as imperfect as I am, to love me. I won't leave her here alone. So, deal with Megan and the

Overlord; then free my family to return to the Earth Realm."

The unicorn shifter's eyes watered. "I am sorry, but your father didn't survive the battle. All of your siblings have changed in ways that won't allow them passage to the Earth Realm, but they will take their places as protectors of the Earth Realm, as will you. You all are the Vigilant; because of your service here, upon your deaths, you will have eternal life as your creator sees fit."

"What of the Overlord?"

"What, is he still alive! Ouch!" Megan was dropped into the throne room at the feet of the Oracle.

Reece touched her mind and said her name, *"Itichicka."*

As Megan started to rise, she fell to her knees, tears falling uncontrollably from her eyes. She stared at Reece. *"You said my name! I am powerless now. How'd you know?"*

"I've known a long time. Remember, I told you I would make you pay for threatening my family? Do what you are told – and I'll let you live. The moment you try to manipulate me or mine again, I will end you."

Megan shivered, and Reece narrowed his gaze, daring her to tell anyone what he'd threatened.

The Oracle placed the pendant around her neck. Megan cowered away from it but was pushed down by an invisible force. Her lips were stuck together, and she was unable to speak. The Oracle placed a hand on her head. Megan shook her head to get away but was held in place by the unicorn shifter's magic. The green glow flowed over Megan's body, changing her warrior clothes to a white and gold-trimmed gown.

"Release him. "The Oracle pointed to the Overlord.

Reece let go of the Overlord's beast. The unicorn shifter placed a hand on the beast's head. The Overlord transformed from beast to man in a regal but modest white and gold-trimmed shirt and pants.

The Oracle snapped her fingers. "Wake!"

"What's wrong with him?" Reece stepped back from them.

"I am telepathically using the spell from the *Book of Magic Transfer.* Its spell will hold him until I complete what has to be done. I will bring harmony and peace back to The Void and ensure the safety of the Earth Realm."

"I want Megan to pay for what she did to my family." Reece crossed his arms.

"Oh, she will pay, and so will he. But you have a price to pay also."

"I understand. You want me to stay here as protector. I can do that willingly."

"You are also to stay here as the final law. Your rule as the law has to be just to keep the balance. Upon the last day of your purpose, you may be gifted what all Vigilant and servants of the Order of Melchizedek are gifted from the Creator of All."

"I can accept that." Reece sighed and stood to the side.

"Now, only you are strong enough to hold their hands together during the ceremony."

Reece grabbed each of them by the wrist and forced their hands to clasp together. "Like this?"

"Perfect." The unicorn shifter nodded then nailed her gaze upon the Overlord. "You have misused your gift and perverted the prophecy of your coming by killing the woman with a kind heart and pure soul who was chosen for you. Our world almost came to ruin that day as she defended herself against your greed for power and control of what was never meant to be yours. Therefore, I, and the other ancients, found you another wife. One who is equally powerful, selfish, and greedy– but she is greedy for love, family, home, and belongings – everything you have taken from her. You have kidnapped her father and turned him into one of your Sandmen. You used him to torture the dreams of magicals and humans you want to manipulate. Her father is free now, one of the only full Rumpelstiltskins alive, and because Megan is part Rumpelstiltskin, he is allowed to take his role with the ancients and is in agreement with your punishment."

The Overlord's mouth opened. "How dare you! I will not be forced to bond with this shrew who's tried to kill me and destroy everything I've worked hard to build. I will destroy the Earth Realm as it has been the cause of all the pain I've endured since I took my place as ruler."

The Oracle snapped her fingers, and the Overlord's power to speak was muffled again.

"You put the blame for your parents' death at your late wife's feet? It was your greed and arrogance that caused their deaths, along with your unborn child. You attempted to yank the power stone that was embedded within her from her cold body. In your anger, you lashed out at the dragons, almost killing them to extinction. Your punishment is just. You will lose your strength and power to wield magic as it will reside within the nether until you fall in love with your wife. Each day you grow to love her and respect the power you were given; you will be gifted with more of your magic. If you retreat, the magic will leave you, but if you stand fast, you will be granted a child with your wife."

Megan was given the freedom to speak. "I will never accept his love! He imprisoned my father, which led my mother to starve herself to death. I will hate him with all within me until I die. He was reckless and would have seen all of us magicals thrown into the fire prison lake with our ancestors. If hating him keeps us safe, I will hate him forever. I will never lie with him to bear him children — never!"

"You will marry him, and he will have to earn every bit of your love, but once his love is returned, you will bear many children for him. Your magic will also be restrained, and until you both are of one accord, it will disperse equally in the nether. Remember this: If you or the Overlord seek to take the magicals to war against the Earth Realm again, you will die. The magic in the nether will go to your offspring equally or will find another host worthy of the treaty made that keeps all of us from facing a worse fate than our ancestors."

Jeb handed the Oracle a scepter. She touched the Overlord then Megan with the tip of it. The queen's crown was placed on Megan's head as the Oracle spoke words in an ancient tongue. Magic from the Overlord and Megan rose from their bodies in a blue and orange hue, and a black orb of darkness that seemed to go on forever opened above their heads to absorb it.

The Oracle lifted the scepter and handed it to Jeb. Then Wykwor stepped forward with a sword that glowed.

"This is the sword Merlin bargained for—the sword of Excalibur. It is to knight those who are sacred protectors of the veil. The former queen will always remain the veil between the Earth Realm and The Void. She needs warriors who can fill the gap, be the gatekeepers in those places her veil doesn't reach. You, all with your mates, will serve that purpose as a Vigilant."

Reece looked at each one of his siblings. All of them had changed. All had found love through the journey that could have broken them. He would make his father proud and be the Vigilant to keep their home and family safe.

The ceremony was over. The King and Queen of The Void were arguing already. The Vigilant guards escorted the Overlord to one side of the castle. Megan sobbed as she was escorted to another wing of the court.

Reece grabbed Ora's hand. He bent and whispered to her, "I am strong enough for your magic. Will you be forever my mate?"

"Yes, forever." Ora lifted her lips to his.

This time, Reece felt the force of her magic in the kiss. His lips tingled, and he inhaled. It was sweet and delicious. Wrapping his arms around hers, he told her *I love you.*

Epilogue

The Lewis clan built themselves a place just outside Newport, RI, the mirage town for humans. Reece had been fully trained for his role and was allowed to finish high school with Ora. Ora managed the school paper and the underground news gossip source for magicals. Many years passed. The forest behind their family gym had become the headquarters for the Vigilant, who kept order at the borders of The Void and the Earth Realm. Their mother remained the owner and coach for many sports teams in town. Later, Reece and Ora were married and moved to their building at the border of HellTown where rogue magicals lived. His sister EmVee and her husband became coaches at the high school for football and boxing. Dexter and his wife were travelers who could go to the Earth and The Void to transport humans and magicals. His sister Rei and her husband moved back to the Earth Realm and protected that side from invasion while training worthy Vigilant for Reece's and Jeb's team.

❋ ❋ ❋

The Dragon moved through the air at top speed. It approached the Mount of Desolation where dragons were banished after the Overlord became king. He landed on the snow-covered mountaintop and transformed into a male form resembling a human. His other dragonkin couldn't transform. It was to them a curse that one could, but in this, he would gain their acceptance.

As he walked through the cave's entrance, his eyes adjusted to the light of the fire from the lava flowing through the mountain at the feet of their king dragon.

"Your highness, I have good news." Rawrick bowed.

"What is it?"

"The Protector Reece Lewis' children were stolen. The Overlord has been framed as the orchestrator."

"Why should this please me?"

"It is because of Reece Lewis that the Overlord still lives. Our plan to incite him to war with the Earth Realm was diverted by this Reece Lewis, now the Protector, even stronger than the Overlord. He doesn't know about our kind and that we still live in exile. We can use his children, who we kidnapped, as leverage, a bargaining tool, a way to manipulate him to our will. He would kill the Overlord as it is said that he and the Cambion he married were never to have children but had triplets."

"Very well. Go to the Protector and fill his head with the lies that the Overlord has orchestrated this plan. Demand the Overlord's death."

"That, I will."

THE END

L.M. Preston

See what happens to Reece and Ora's children in 2024 Release of The Misfits Series

Please leave a review, and visit my website at www.lmpreston.com

ALSO BY L.M. PRESTON

FICTION

2024 MISFITS

Continuation of the Vigilant Series

Lost

Frigid

Unlucky

VIGILANT SERIES

Insatiable Darkness	*Book 0*
Caged Fire	*Book 1*
Unbreakable Darkness	*Book 1.5*
Scepter Of Fire	*Book 2*
Break The Darkness	*Book 2.5*
Rebel of Fire	*Book 3*
Sword of Darkness	*Book 3.5*
Blade Of Fire	*Book 4*

Spinoff Series based in this world 2024

PURGATORY REIGN SERIES

Purgatory Reign	*Book 1*
Deviant Storm	*Book 2*
Colliding Souls	
Fierce Tides	*Book 3*

THE PACK SERIES

The Pack	*Book 1*
Retribution	*Book 2*

THE BANDITS SERIES

Bandits	*Book 1*
Wastelands	*Book 2*
Double Trouble Luv	
Thundering Luv	
Flutter of Luv	

STANDALONES

Flutter Of Luv

Thundering Luv

Double Trouble Luv

NON FICTION

Building Your Empowered Steps

Homeschooling and Working While

Raising Amazing Learners

Team Wave Surfing

www.ingramcontent.com/pod-product-compliance
Lightning Source LLC
Chambersburg PA
CBHW071256250626
47159CB00004B/1204